SAROS COWASJEE is Professor Emeritus at the University of Regina. A graduate of the universities of Agra and Leeds (U. K.), he worked for two years with the Times of India Press, Mumbai, before leaving for Canada. His fictional works are *Goodbye to Elsa* (1974), *Nude Therapy* (1979), *The Last of the Maharajas* (screenplay, 1980), and *'Strange Meeting' and Other Stories* (2005). Among others, he has written books on Sean O'Casey and Mulk Raj Anand, and edited a number of Raj fiction anthologies, including *The Oxford Anthology of Raj Stories* (1998) and *A Raj Collection* (2005).

~

'Written in the first person, [the novel] tells the humorous story of an Anglo-Indian professor on leave from a "midwest" university . . . . It has a strong plot with crazed twists ending in the protagonist holed up with his sweetheart's baby held hostage as he negotiates with the police in a comical turn reminiscent of the finale of Nabokov's Despair. *As the illiterati say, it's a hoot.'*

The Review of Books, Toronto

'The story is, in reality, a modern tragedy rather than a social comedy, though this is not always apparent for the writing is laced with light, satiric touches rather than heavy, trenchant criticism.'

World Literature Today, Norman, Oklahoma

Other Books by Saros Cowasjee

FICTION

Goodbye to Elsa
~
Nude Therapy
~
The Last of the Maharajas (screenplay)
~
'Strange Meeting' and Other Stories
~
Modern Indian Fiction (ed.)
~
Modern Indian Short Stories (ed.)
~
Stories from the Raj (ed.)
~
More Stories from the Raj and After (ed.)
~
When the British Left (ed.)
~
The Raj and After (ed.)
~
Women Writers of the Raj (ed.)
~
Orphans of the Storm: Stories on the Partition of India (ed.)
~
The Best Short Stories of Flora Annie Steel (ed.)
~
The Oxford Anthology of Raj Stories (ed.)
~
A Raj Collection (ed.)
~
The Mulk Raj Anand Omnibus (ed.)
~
Mulk Raj Anand: Selected Short Stories (ed.)

CRITICISM

Sean O'Casey: The Man Behind the Plays
~
O'Casey
~
Coolie: An Assessment
~
So Many Freedoms: A Study of the Major Fiction of Mulk Raj Anand
~
Author to Critic: The Letters of Mulk Raj Anand (ed.)
~
Studies in Indian and Anglo-Indian Fiction

My Dear Maura

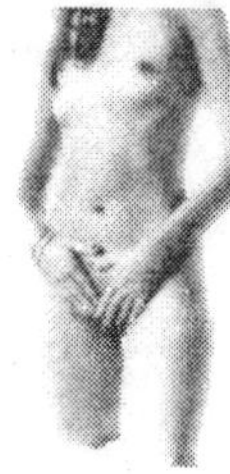

Saros Cowasjee

VISION BOOKS
(Incorporating Orient Paperbacks)
New Delhi • Mumbai • Hyderabad

www.vision**books**india.com

The picture on the cover is from a print where the name of the artist has been obliterated. We thus apologise for not being able to acknowledge copyright, but shall gladly do so if the artist or his representative should contact us.
(The Publisher)

Earlier published as
The Assistant Professor
by TSAR (Toronto & Oxford)

ISBN 81-7094-646-8

Published by
Vision Books Pvt. Ltd.
(Incorporating Orient Paperbacks & CARING imprints)
24 Feroze Gandhi Road, Lajpat Nagar III
New Delhi-110024, India.
Phone: (+91-11) 2983 6470
Fax: (+91-11) 2983 6490
E-mail: visionbk@vsnl.com

Printed at
Rashtra Rachna Printers
C-88, Ganesh Nagar, Pandav Nagar Complex
Delhi-110092, India.

To the memory of Mulk Raj Anand

1

I met Maura Hawkins at a nude marathon in Corwind, a small town a few miles north of Erigon. It was organized by a psychologist called Julien Wolfe, who had been given a large sum of money by the National Research Council to study the effects of physical nudity on group interaction. He had rented Mountain View for the purpose: the farmhouse where I had spent six months meditating on questions of life and death some two years ago.

Wolfe wanted only twenty participants—ten men and ten women. So he did not put an ad in the papers. But the news of the marathon spread like a prairie fire and it took him eight weeks to choose the candidates from the hundreds of applicants from all over the province who wanted to take their pants off. Being a man with a normal penis, I thought I would never be selected. But my psychiatrist, Dr Clifford Enright, recommended me as a "unique phenomenon." Besides, there were two berths reserved for faculty members, most of whom were too shy to take their jackets off except when calling on the wives of their colleagues.

Mountain View was exactly as I had left it. The only apparent changes were the mattresses strewn all over the place and the kitchen stacked with cases of beer and bologna sandwiches. The curtains were drawn and we were asked to resist the temptation of peeping out. For thirty-six hours, starting at six p.m., our job was, in the words of Julien Wolfe, "to take off our social masks, stop playing games, and start interacting authentically and transparently." Hugging, kissing and defecating were permitted, but intercourse and the fondling of genitals were strictly forbidden.

At five minutes to six, Mr Wolfe opened the door of the house to the participants, some of whom had been waiting outside since the early afternoon. Wolfe was a stout, red-faced man of about fifty. He wore sandals, a yellow turtle-neck sweater which stretched like a corset over his protuberant belly, and a simulated leather jacket. I wondered what he would be like in the nude. He guessed as much, for the first thing he told us was that he wasn't going to undress—that as a therapist he had to maintain the professional distance so necessary if he were to help others. This seemed reasonable to me, though it didn't dampen my curiosity.

No sooner had we sat down in a circle in the living room, than people began to unbutton their clothes. Wolfe urged us to be patient and assured us there would be plenty of time to show ourselves in the nude. There were certain things he would like to make clear before the ultimate revelation. As some were sweating to take their clothes off, he threatened to turn the thermostat down to 10° C. Since Canadians love heat, this had a cooling effect on the more zealous participants and they elected to keep their clothes on for a while.

"Friends," began Wolfe. "Our first task is to say a small prayer for the National Research Council for making this occasion possible. The food you will eat, the beer you will drink, the mattresses on which you will rest your tired bodies, all, all have been paid for by the Council."

"Amen!" said half a dozen voices. They wanted to get over with the thanksgiving as quickly as possible. Some began to undo their buttons and laces again.

"Wait," beseeched Wolfe. "We have assembled here to help each other, to find answers to our individual problems. Our problems may differ, in fact they do differ, but not the source. The truth is that our problems lie in our betrayal of the primeval state of man. We imprison ourselves in a fortress of clothes and thereby separate ourselves from our animal brethren. Except humans, no living creature suffers estrangement, fantasies and emotional upheavals. Clothes are Satan's most insidious weapon to lead us to our damnation. They hide what is most beautiful in man and woman."

"Whoop!" cried a pretty housewife, standing up and taking off her bra and swinging it in circles over her head as if it were a lasso. She finally let go the bra which sailed across the room and caught Wolfe full in the face. People clapped their hands and cheered, while the housewife stood like a victorious general with her hands on her hips and her head cocked to one side. She had very thin arms and legs, and no breasts at all.

Wolfe pleaded with the group again. "Please, ladies and gentlemen, please give me two more minutes."

"You have them," said a fat man, scratching his balls.

"Nakedness is the mighty leveller of class distinctions. It takes us back to the state in which we entered the world, and to the state in which we must exist. Nudity is the common denominator that binds mankind together, even though one's ass may be hanging or one's belly sticking out. Only through disrobing completely can the two sexes meet on an equal footing and see each other as they really are. There is nothing more democratic than nudity; with their trappings off, everyone is equal . . ."

Wolfe asked for another two minutes, but this time he didn't get them. We hadn't left our families behind to come to a lecture, and the housewife, who had earlier flung the bra, now wriggled out of her panties. Within seconds all were standing naked, gaping at each other and smacking their lips. I stood shivering. However, what angered me was that there was nothing democratic about nudity. Never before had I seen such an assortment of genitals. As a Social Democrat it pained my conscience and I could not help feeling that Wolfe was a damned swindler. "Everyone is equal," were his last words. "Where?" I felt like asking. The man standing next to me had a penis twice as big as mine.

Wolfe gave us two hours in which to eat and drink and get to know each other. With beer and sandwiches in their hands, a roomful of people screamed and yelled and talked and talked in a huge effort to communicate. I had absolutely no desire to mingle with this carnal-minded crowd, and I could not for the life of me see what their problems were and what good it could do them to be standing in the nude. Wolfe told me that the group comprised four farmers, two social workers, two professors, a politician, an artist, and a number of housewives. The professors were obviously Horace Peabody and myself, and I sought Horace out from the crowd. He was pacing the floor with a pipe in his mouth and a pencil and a scroll in his hands. Behind his ear was tucked a goose-quill pen. He shrugged me off, saying, "Get thee hence to thy wedded one," and twisting his handle-bar moustache he ambled away in his peculiar, shuffling gait. I was hurt, though I knew he had nothing personal against me but was waiting for his poetic muse to appear. Barring myself, he was the most dignified person in the group and along with me the only man with a sleepy penis. The rest of the penises were in various stages of erection, and the higher they rose the more vociferous their owners became.

At the end of the two hours, Wolfe asked us to assemble in the living room for what he called the Peak Stimulation Experience. He issued us black paper goggles with elastic bands that we were to wear while choosing our partners for the remainder of the evening. The goggles were something like those an optometrist makes his patients wear while testing their eyes: they had pin-holes in them which limited the vision to a radius of one foot. We were asked to wear the goggles and concentrate on the genitals of a person of the opposite sex which we found most comfortable and relaxing. Only after we had chosen the most relaxing genitals were we to look up and see the face of the person. If there was mutual agreement, it had to be signified by putting one's tongue out.

The men and women formed two separate rows, facing each other at a distance of about ten feet. I looked from one pudendum to another, and to my utter astonishment found that they all looked alike, except for the hue and colour of the hair. And then my eyes came to rest on a vulva which didn't have a single hair to obstruct the vision. I looked up and saw that the person was the same housewife who had swung the bra. To make myself acceptable and to rise in her esteem, I began to tickle my genitals in an effort to brighten them. She saw my fears and smiled as if to say, "Don't worry."

When Wolfe asked us if we were ready, the housewife spoke for me with a modest yes. She turned out to be my Maura.

No sooner were we paired than we were asked to find for ourselves a quiet corner in the house. We were urged to lay bare our souls to our partners, but under no circumstances to have intercourse or fondle each others genitals.

"Would kissing sex be considered as fondling?" I asked, being a stickler for rules.

"Yes," snarled Wolfe.

A few laughed at my question, a farmer thumped me on the back and said, "Lad, ye don't ask them things," and Horace Peabody coughed in disapproval. I turned around to see his partner. God! she must have been eighty inches in the hips! My Horace who weighs a little over a hundred pounds! I would have thought it all a mistake but for the fact that he was trying to get his arm round her waist and could only reach as far as her arse. The goose-quill pen was still tucked behind his ear, but his pipe and his scroll lay on the floor.

As I knew the house well, I was able to direct Maura to a spot where the two of us could converse unseen. In the basement, behind the furnace, I unrolled a sleeping-bag on which we sat down. Maura folded her arms over her breasts and drew up her knees. I was surprised and asked her how she, who had swung the bra over her head, could now be bashful.

"I don't know," she said meditatively. "Something came over me . . . I just felt liberated. I'm usually a very shy person. I've never done anything like this before. But I suppose I'd always wanted to."

"What you did was right," I said. "Besides, you don't need bras, anyway."

"If you don't like me the way I am, you can find yourself another girl," she retorted, her eyes spitting fire.

"I love you, Maura."

"You men love too easily."

"Not me. Lie down, Maura, and let me prove my love for you."

She lay down on her back, and the ritual began. I took her feet in my two hands and pressed them together and kissed them. I kissed her toes several times and then I moved up, inch by inch, kissing the length of her legs till I came to her sex. From there I took the bypass, continued the journey from the naval upwards. I paused awhile on her breasts, neck, chin, and lips. I rested on her lips, rubbing my nose against her nose, licking her eyes. Her eye-lashes glistening with my saliva. It took me about ten minutes. I didn't have a watch to time it.

After the loving and kissing, I put my head between her thighs and got my first full view of her vagina. It had the expression of a new-born baby crying. My heart went out to it and I gently covered it with my hand and christened it, "My handful of love."

"That's enough," said Maura, sitting up. "We're here to unburden our souls and you go about doing funny things to me. Why not tell me something about yourself. Are you married?"

"You unburden first. Are you married?"

"Yes."

"Where's your husband?"

"At home."

"And he allowed you to come here?"

"Allowed me? We're separated."

"Where does he live?"

"In the same house. Clare and I—Clare's my daughter—live on the ground floor and he lives upstairs."

"A strange arrangement."

"You see, Ralph doesn't earn much. He's a carpenter. And it's cheaper this way. He lives his own life and I live mine. What about you?"

"I'll tell you later—it has to be sorted out. What went wrong with your marriage?"

"Oh, everything. He was all right as long as there were just the two of us. But then I had the baby, and he started hating it and started going out with other girls. Said he never wanted to be a father, and that Clare wasn't his. So . . . I don't want to talk about it."

"*Procreare liberos lepidum est onus,*" I said.

"What's that?"

"Begetting children is a delightful duty."

"You tell that to him."

"I will, I will."

"He drinks, too, and used to be on drugs till the police found out. But that's not why I left him. He is a saliromaniac—that's what Dr Enright calls him."

"Dr Clifford Enright! He's my doctor."

"He's ours, too. Ralph would take my clothes and Clare's and scatter them on the floor and trample on them and spit and urinate on them, all the while abusing me. He did it regularly . . ."

"Did you also go to Dr Enright?"

"Yes, he referred me here."

"For what?"

" I don't know. He said it might do me some good. How did you get here?"

"Well," I began. I didn't know what to say. "There's really nothing wrong with me."

"If there weren't, you wouldn't be here."

"You're right; you're very right, Maura. We are mad to be here—in the midst of these freaks. Wolfe is a psychotic, a Peeping Tom, with his talk of nakedness being the great leveller. He has gathered here fetishists, frotteurs, homosexuals, prostitutes and heaven knows what. Let's get out of this place fast, and as quietly as we can."

"But how? Our clothes are upstairs."

"Damn the clothes. There is not a moment to lose. It's now or never. Follow me."

We climbed out of the basement window, jumped over the fence, and ran to my car. Maura wanted to go back and fetch her clothes, but I told her to desist—we would be caught. I started the motor, and with a roar and a tremendous spinning of wheels over the gravel we shot into the moonlight. We had just taken a turn onto the paved road when an RCMP cruiser came behind us and flashed its red beacon. "Amen! Amen!" I said several times before I turned to Maura and gasped, "Why the police?"

"You haven't your lights on," she said looking straight ahead of her.

"Oh God," I sighed. This indeed was the end. I closed my eyes and I could see the banner headlines in the local paper, NUDE PROFESSOR WOOS BY MOONLIGHT.

The police and I come frequently in contact, and I generally step out of my car to greet them and make them feel important. But for once I sat still.

The officer came up and without looking at me asked for my driver's licence and registration, I opened the glove compartment and gave them to him. After scrutinizing, he handed them back and asked, "Have you been drinking, sir?"

"Nope."

"May I search your car?" he said, pointing his flashlight at the front seat. The full beam fell on Maura's vulva. He stepped back; he couldn't believe it.

"What's going on here?" he asked, stupefied.

"Nothing," I said.

He looked at me. I looked at him. He looked hard at me. I could see the expresion on his face change from that of suspicion to one of incredulity. "Professor Tristan Elliott, sir," he said with a broad grin.

"That's correct."

"I'm Gordon Turner, sir. I took a class from you."

"Turner?" I said, looking up at a chubby-faced young man with doughnut crumbs around his mouth. "I remember you well, Turner. I gave you an A, didn't I?"

"No, sir, you gave me a C."

My hopes were dashed. "There is no peace, saith the Lord, unto the wicked," I mumbled.

Turner spoke out of turn, "I enjoyed your class, though."

"Turner."

"Sir."

"Turner."

"Sir, what has happened to you? Have you been robbed? Assaulted? Do you need help?"

"Turner, I need a pair of trousers and something for this lady here."

"But, sir, I must know what has happened. This is most unusual."

"Turner, we have not committed any of the seven deadly sins nor have we broken one of the Ten Commandments. Is your professor's word not good enough for you? You were my best student, Turner!"

"But . . ."

"Just get me a pair of trousers, Turner, and stop butting around."

"From where, sir?"

"Don't you carry a spare one? In your profession!"

"No, sir."

"Then see me home."

"That I will, sir. Where do you live?"

"River Heights. Off Broadway."

"Follow me," he said, getting into the car.

I followed the police car as it sped along the highway with its beacon flashing. When we reached the outskirts of Erigon, Turner turned on the siren to get us post-haste through red lights and stop signs. The police escort and the speed at which we were travelling made me feel as if I were the President of the

United States.

To avoid detection, we took the stairs to my sixth floor apartment. I asked Maura to spend the night there—in the morning I would go the the Army and Navy store and buy her a dress in which to go home. She could sleep on my bed while I would make the best of the sofa. Just as I was dozing off, Maura called from the bedroom: "Tristan, why didn't we tell Mr Wolfe we were leaving? Why did we leave our clothes behind?"

"I don't know, darling," I said half in sleep. "I guess there would have been no harm had we done so."

"Then why? Why this running naked in the middle of the night?"

"I don't know. I think it just came over me—it had to be done this way."

"What?" she yelled.

"Maura, why did a modest girl like you have to take off your bra and fling it in Wolfe's face?"

"Why?" And after a longish pause, she added, "I understand, Tristan. Good night."

2

When I got up in the morning, Maura was sound asleep. She was lying flat on her back in a lotus position: the legs crossed, the arms stretched on either side of her, and the palms turned up. Her lips were slightly ajar, and as she purred gently her unassertive nipples rose and fell. As for the rest of her body, to quote the poet, "It beggar'd all description." And I realized that once again I was in love.

My Maura deserved the best clothes money could buy. But I didn't have her size. Admiring her beautiful body, it struck me how very alike we were physically, except that I was four inches taller and two inches broader. That then was her size, and I hastened to the store.

I went straight to the women's section and said good morning to a middle-aged female assistant who also bore some physical resemblance to me. She did not return my greetings but said that the men's wear was at the back. I told her it was women's I needed and that too the best.

"What size are these pantyhose?" I asked, picking up a slim packet which showed a woman standing on one leg and kicking the other way above her head.

"They're all one size," she answered.

I didn't quite understand. "Do you have one that's open; I'd like to try it on."

"What do you mean?"

"I need it for a lady . . . something my size, though not as big."

"This should fit. It stretches."

"And if it doesn't?—I mean if it doesn't fit her."

She gave me an ugly look—quite effortlessly. She was probably one of those Canadian bitches who wants to keep Canada white, though I with three-fourths British blood in me had a better title to this land than the continental porridge that she was. I didn't want to argue with her; I asked her to put it in a bag for me, and turned to the more important item.

"Could you show me a dress? I like the yellow one there."

"What size?" she asked.

"The same. Two inches too tight for me."

"What's your size?"

"I don't know. Could you measure me?"

"Certainly not," she said loudly.

"No need to shout, madam. I'm not deaf."

But she had spoken for the benefit of the manager, who walked up to us slowly and cautiously as if he were suffering from an attack of the piles. He inquired of the assistant what the matter was and I could see that she had had a lot to whisper in his ears.

After the assistant left, the manager turned to me. He kept looking at me and shaking his head. Then he spread out his hands as if there was nothing more to say. His pantomime unnerved me and I would have gladly foregone the dress and left with the pantyhose. But I hadn't paid for it, and the occasion demanded that I said something brave.

"Well," I said.

"What's your problem, sir?" he asked.

I told him that I wanted to buy a dress for a lady, but the assistant would neither measure me nor allow me to try on a dress. I told him that a lady was waiting for clothes to go home in. This last admission made it incumbent on me to tell him how she came to be naked, and his tiny eyes glowed. Suddenly the picture of Maura in a lotus position came before my eyes and all I wanted now was to run back and cover her with kisses.

"Let's see what we can do for you," he said, moving towards the counter. "You say you don't have the lady's size."

"Give me anything—anything that's too tight for me." And I looked at my watch; I had been away for almost an hour.

He wanted to measure me, show me some of his latest designs. He wanted to know more about the nude marathon and how one qualified for it. He said he wouldn't mind paying a hundred bucks to get in. But I was sweating to get back. I paid for the yellow dress and the panty-hose and asked him to keep the change. He yelled back that he was no cab driver.

When I got back, I put the keys gently into the door. I wanted to catch Maura exactly as I had left her; I wanted to do something (I now forget what) which no man has ever done to his sweetheart. I stole into the bedroom. There was no one there. The bed was made; there was no evidence that anybody had slept in it. I became frantic: I looked under the bed, behind the sofa, in the closets, everywhere. For once I regretted that there weren't more closets in the apartment I could search. Where had she gone? and how? She couldn't have fled naked! She might have got into my clothes—but no, my two pairs of trousers and three shirts were still hanging. I looked around to see if she had left a note or something: some sign or token that she had been here. But there was nothing.

I missed a heartbeat as it crossed my mind that I might have been hallucinating. Could it be that there never was a Maura? That there never was a marathon? That I had all along been dreaming? If so, then it was my end and I might as well say goodbye to sanity now as later. But I must check the facts; I should phone and ask Horace about the marathon.

I dialed. Priscilla, his wife, answered. She said her hubby hadn't been home since Friday, and asked if I knew where he could be. I had the presence of mind to drop the phone from my hand.

My talk with Priscilla gave me some assurance that the marathon had indeed taken place and was no figment of my imagination. Horace had been there with his pipe and scroll, and had taken off with the fat arse to write his "divorce poems." But what of Maura? Why? I could phone and find out.

I picked up the telephone directory. There were some twenty Hawkinses in Erigon, but none with the name of Maura. I phoned them all—from A to Z. The closest I came was Miss Mona Hawkins in Santa Maria Senior Citizens' Home. She swore she knew nothing about the marathon and had not slept in my bed and that if I didn't hang up immediately she would send for the police.

My heart sank. Enright was right, after all. I was a sure victim of hallucinations. I sat down on the sofa and began thinking how best I could put an end to this life. I decided I would go down to the second floor and jump to my death. Jumping from the sixth floor would break every bone in my body and mutilate me beyond recognition.

Just then a smell wafted from the bathroom. I got up to see what it was. In the toilet a turd was floating, seven-eighths under water like an iceberg. So Maura had been here—she had graced my apartment and I was not dreaming. For a moment I even forgot my Maura at the joy of discovering that I was sane, absolutely sane.

I was about to flush the toilet when I thought I had better keep some proof of Maura's visit before I started doubting my sanity again. I got my Brownie and pulled out the black-and-white film and rolled on a colour. Then I took six shots from six different angles. After that, I pressed the lever and saw the turd pirouette before it got sucked up into the whirlpool.

"*Au revoir*, not farewell," I said triumphantly.

3

It was five when I awoke. There was light outside. The days are getting longer, and I am getting lonelier. It's four days I have not been out. I have been waiting for Maura to come or to call me. Yesterday the phone rang three times. It was the same man who got the number wrong three times. He at least had a number he could dial. What if it was wrong? I had nothing. No, that wasn't true.

I phoned the weather office. Southerly winds gusting to sixty with light showers in the evening. I phoned the stores. They would be open till nine tonight. I phoned Air Canada. All flights arriving and departing on time. I phoned Dr Clifford Enright. Yes, I could come and see him.

The doctor was waiting for me. He was a tall, thin Englishman with bifocals. I don't know why he wore those glasses, for he never looked at his patients through them but from around the edges of the rims. His nose was always screwed up as if the whole world stank. He pointed to a chair and asked me how I was.

"I'm very lonely," I said.

"We are all very lonely," he said in a bored voice. "Have you been writing?"

I told him that I had written about the marathon he had sent me to, but because I left early my report was incomplete.

"What marathon?"

"The one in Corwind with Julien Wolfe."

"Ah," he said, brightening up. "Tell me all about it."

I told him that I had never been more disgusted in my life. To my mind Julien Wolfe was a fraud and the crowd that he had collected the most carnal-minded I had ever seen.

"Doctor!" I exclaimed, as I recalled that he had also referred Maura to Wolfe. "Doctor, do you know Maura Hawkins?"

"Yes."

"Could I have her phone number?"

"Why?"

"She was at the marathon. We left together."

"But why do you want her number? Besides, I am not supposed to divulge the phone numbers of my patients."

"Doctor," I said, looking him straight in his eyes. "We are in love with each other."

"Now, now Tristan."

"It's true. Do you want me to . . .?"

"All right," he said, putting his feet up on the desk and leaning back in his swivel chair.

I narrated everything exactly as it had taken place from the time we put on the goggles and selected each other as partners till the time I returned from the store and flushed the toilet. He listened to me with his palms cupped over his mouth and his eyes peering from above the top of the glasses. After I had done, he straightened himself in the chair and said he had a few questions to ask me, and I should consider my answers very carefully before I opened my mouth.

"Now Tristan, do you think it was the right thing to run naked from the therapy session?"

"Yup," I said.

"Think. Think before you answer. Why was it right?"

"It wasn't right."

"And why wasn't it right?"

"Because there was no need for it. We were not prisoners; we could have gone upstairs, taken our clothes and told Mr Wolfe that we didn't feel like participating any more."

"Had you had done so, there would have been none of the problems that followed. You see how one problem leads to another. One has to act smartly the first time. Now, you agree that running out naked was a mistake. Then why did you do it?"

"Let me think," I said.

"That's an improvement, Tristan. I want you to think. I want you to think and tell me why you did such a foolish thing."

"Something came over me. All the avenues seemed closed. It seemed we were trapped—that there was no way out. That if we didn't run we would . . ."

"Yes."

"I think it was my loathing of everything that was taking place there. It was the beastliness and vulgarity of the Canadians."

"Don't turn the issue into something racial. It could have happened in India."

"No, it couldn't."

"All right, let's get back to the subject."

I thought for a while. What I had done seemed terribly stupid now. Yet at the time it seemed the only sensible thing. "Why had I run naked?" I had no satisfactory explanation and I told Dr Enright so.

"I'm glad, Tristan, that you make no excuses, but acknowledge your mistake. 'Not to know' is the first step towards self-knowledge. We often act on impulse and then look for a reason to justify our action. It is wrong to find motives for things that happen because of a sheer perversity of will. Do you agree?"

I told him I couldn't agree with him more, that left to myself I would never have thought of going to the marathon. I asked him why he had sent me there. He said he would tell me that some other time—it would be better if today he were to ask questions and I were to confine myself to answering them.

"Tristan, there are two other questions I'd like to ask you," he began. "The first is: do you think it was proper to try on a lady's dress in the store?"

"I did not try it on," I answered.

"But you wanted to."

"I did not insist."

"That was intelligent of you. But you wanted to try the dress on. Is that correct?"

"Yes."

"Why?"

"Because I didn't have Maura's size. And I couldn't send her home naked."

"I know that Tristan."

"Then why do you ask?"

"A man does not try on a lady's dress in a store."

"What was I supposed to do? Pick up anything from the rack?"

"Yes."

"I wanted to give her a dress not simply good enough to get home in, but something that would be worthy of my love for her. Are you going to give me her phone number or not?"

Dr Enright picked up a pencil and began jabbing holes in a piece of paper. After a few seconds, he spoke: "Let's simplify this. Do you think you made a sensible request to the store attendant?"

"I don't know. It was necessary if the dress was to fit her. What would you have done in such a situation?"

"I wouldn't have been in such a situation."

"Nor would I, had you not sent me to the marathon. Why did you send me there? Why can't you answer my question now?"

Dr Enright smiled, then checked himself. He put the paper and pencil away and addressed me in a tone marked with gravity.

"Tristan, this dress business is more silly than profitable to be pursued any further. But I am quite worried about your taking photographs of the turd. I have never heard of such a thing before. Will you tell me why you had to do this?"

I explained that when I returned with the clothes and found my flat empty, I panicked. I suddenly felt that I might have been hallucinating—that it was he who first put the idea into my head that I was given to hallucinations. The turd floating was my only evidence that Maura had been with me and that I was not dreaming.

"But you don't go about photographing turds," Dr Enright interjected with some impatience.

"As far as I can see she left no fingerprints," I said with mounting temper. "Besides, I don't go about photographing turds, I photographed a turd."

"Oh, I see!"

"If I hadn't, you would have insisted I was hallucinating. Wouldn't you?"

He appeared stumped, but returned to the attack. But I could see that he no longer had a logical position to support his assertion.

"You should not have photographed it," was all he could say.

"What was I to do, then? I could have taken it out and put it in a beaker, but I didn't have a pair of tongs. And you wouldn't have approved of that either."

"No, I wouldn't. How am I to tell you that what you did was not normal?"

"Doctor, don't you see that the photograph is the only evidence I have of my sanity—the one evidence that Maura had been to my place and I wasn't dreaming? But I needn't have used a colour film."

"What?" he burst out, squeezing his eyes shut.

"I took out the black-and-white and put in colour."

"You did!"

"Yes. It was very foolish of me and I apologize."

"No, Tristan, if you are to shoot pictures of turds you might as well use colour. Take an appointment from my secretary for next Thursday; no, see me whenever you feel the need for it."

And he stood up to signify that the interview was over. He stretched his hand across the table, and I shook it.

"Could I have Maura's phone number, doctor?"

"No."

"I'm in love with her."

"You are not to see her, do you understand? You two are not good for each other."

"Who am I good for?"

"We'll talk about it when you come again. Goodbye."

"Please give me her number. I can't bear to live without her—I'll kill myself."

"Tristan, a man can kill himself only once."

"You don't believe I can kill myself, do you?"

"Of course I do. But I know you won't do anything so stupid. Though a man who photographs a turd . . ."

He was too obsessed with the turd. "Thank you," I said nonchalantly and walked out of his office in a huff. It had the desired effect, for when I reached home the phone was ringing.

4

"Where have you been, Maura? Why didn't you phone me earlier? I have been waiting for you . . . "

"Don't shout, Tristan. I can hear you."

"But where have you been? Don't you see that I've been waiting for you all these days."

"I phoned you some minutes ago and you weren't in."

"I had gone to Dr Enright to get your number. He wouldn't give it to me."

"Ya, he phoned and said so."

"That was very decent of him," I said bitterly.

"He asked me to phone you."

"Oh, did he? Anyway, hang him. Why did you disappear in the morning?"

"Why did I? You have the nerve to ask me that! Where did you disappear, I'd like to know?"

"I went to the store to get you a dress to go home in. What's your favourite colour?"

"Why?"

"I've bought you a yellow dress. But how did you get home?"

"I got Ralph to come and fetch me."

"No! You had no clothes on you."

"Ralph brought my clothes along."

"No!"

"Stop saying 'no' to everything I say. You didn't think I'd go home naked—did you?"

"No, but God . . . what did he say?"

"Say?"

"Yes, to your being naked in my apartment."

"Nothing. It's none of his business. And it's none of your business either. I've told you that though we live under the same roof, he lives his life and I live mine."

Afraid that she might hang up on me, I quickly asked her to have dinner with me at Sandra's restaurant. She said she couldn't afford a babysitter and that I should drop in at her home after supper—around eight. I didn't relish the idea of running into her husband, but neither could I bear the separation from Maura any longer.

Maura occupied the ground floor of an old, two-storeyed house on University Drive. The top half of the house had been painted green, while the lower half had blotches of red, pink and yellow. Maura was prepared to settle for any colour except green, but Ralph wanted green only. And he had painted his part of the house green and left Maura with a formidable choice of colours. When she asked me what colour she should choose, I suggested green since half the house had already been painted green. She was furious and accused me of siding with her husband against her.

When I knocked, Ralph answered the door."You're the Tristan bloke," he said with a twinkle in his eyes. And he offered me his hand to shake."Yes, very pleased to meet you," I said in my best Leeds accent.

But before I could take his hand he quickly withdrew it. He began to snigger. He next began to laugh. Soon he was convulsed with uncontrollable laughter, bending low and slapping his thighs to the accompaniment of "He, he, he, he." I first thought he was putting on an act to frighten me, but no—there were tears running down his pitted cheeks. After what seemed a long while, he turned around and staggered up the stairs on his stocky legs.

I walked through the passageway into the kitchen. Maura was standing before the sink piled high with the week's dishes. As she briskly scrubbed the pots and plates, she sang a song I have never heard sung more fervently:

I am Woman
Hear me roar
In numbers too big to ignore . . .

Yes I am wise
But it's wisdom born of pain
Yes I've paid the price
But look how much I've gained
If I have to, I can do anything
I am strong
I am invincible
I am woman . . .

"I am Woman," I began to hum as well. And I did considerably well, for I love songs with a martial tune. But Maura continued to ignore me, and I began to feel uneasy.

I looked around. In a corner sat Clare strapped to a potty, looking at me with wide-eyed wonder. I felt drawn towards her as I have never felt towards any other child.

"Is it well with the child?" I asked.

Neither mother nor child responded. Only Maura sang a little more vigorously, and the girl kept looking at me.

"Is it well with the child?" I repeated.

"Better than it is with the mother," Maura retorted. "Take this and dry up the plates." And she threw a dish towel at me.

After the washing and drying, we went into the living room. Maura carried Clare on her potty and placed her in the middle of the room. She then stretched herself on the sofa. I wanted to kiss her and so I came and sat down beside her."Go and sit there," she said firmly, pointing to a chair with a high back. It was a genuine antique. You had to sit on it with your feet firmly planted to the ground, for should you lift your legs the chair would quickly follow suit.

We sat in silence. I did not know what to say or do. I felt

Maura was waiting for me to say something, and that as soon as I said it she would pounce on me. I felt like a rat in a hole—a rat that would, no matter how it leapt, finish up under the cat's paws. I asked:

"Why did your husband laugh at me?"

"You don't have to remind me he's my husband, do you?"

"I'm sorry."

"My husband! Couldn't I be his husband for a change? Must a man always be a husband, and every woman a wife? Can't we change roles for a while? Do cats and dogs have husbands and wives? Why should I be denied my individuality—an individuality that God has given to the female of every species? Couldn't he be Ralph for a day without being my husband?"

"I didn't mean to annoy you—I merely wanted to know why your husband . . . oh, pardon me, I mean Ralph, laughed the way he did."

"You didn't mean to annoy me, but you did!" she sneered. And then with a sigh,"Oh, let it be." Moments later, she spoke again,"He does that to everyone that comes to see me. That's his sense of humour. He did it to Clare, too. She used to cry every time he laughed that way. I asked him to quit or I'd kick his ass for him."

Clare was still sitting on the potty, strapped, but now looking terribly scared. Her mother's outburst had frightened the shit out of her—literally.

"May I kiss Clare?"

"Need you always kiss someone or another?"

"She's a child and needs love."

"OK, but don't lift her."

"I kiss the child for the nurse's sake," I said, getting up and kissing Clare. Clare waved her arms and stuttered,"Dada . . . Dada."

Maura smiled. But when she saw me looking at her she checked herself.

"You've changed," I said.

She did not answer, but looked at me as if she wanted me to

continue.

"You're not the same person I met at the marathon. You don't love me anymore."

"Tristan, I've never been in love with you."

"Oh," I gasped. It had never occurred to me that Maura might not be in love with me. It wasn't that I had taken her love for granted, but I had never thought about it. And I was afraid to think about it now.

"I'm sorry," she said.

I tried to look away from her. I didn't want to meet her eyes.

"I didn't mean to hurt you," she continued.

"That's all right, Maura. I was slipping—it is so easy to slip when one is alone. You put me back on my feet."

"How?"

"When the world turns ugly, our dreams become more beautiful."

I was hoping she wouldn't ask me to explain, for I didn't quite know what I meant, when there was the blare of a saxophone from the top room. Maura stood up and shouted:

"Stop it. Stop it, you beast."

The loud noise turned into a moan. Ralph was emptying his lungs out into the instrument before putting it away.

"You hear that! Playing the saxophone instead of paying the rent. That's my man—that's the man I married for love! There's no food in the house, there isn't money even to buy diapers for the girl. I wanted to ask you over for supper tonight, but I had nothing to give you. He hasn't paid me this month's allowance and he may not pay the next month's either. For myself I don't care, but Clare needs a few things."

"Have you thought of getting a job?"

"I had a job—with *The Hemisphere.* But what job can a woman hold in a man's world? And it's worse if the woman happens to be young and married, with all her eggs gasping for fertilization. At least that's what the editor thought. He couldn't hire me as a reporter for I might become pregnant again, perhaps right in the middle of a news story! So I was hired as a secretary. I naturally resented this, and wrote to the editor pointing out the blatant discrimination against women in the hiring practices of the newspaper. The editor thought that the letter was from one of his readers for the 'Viewpoints' page and passed it on to his assistant. The assistant, like a fool, published it. Next morning the editor realized what had happened. If anybody, he should have fired his assistant for publishing a letter written by one of the employees to the management. Instead he came tearing at me, and shouted: 'You—you can't do that to me. You forget your place—you are just a secretary.' His concern apparently was that he had made an ass of himself, and that I was instrumental in showing him up. I was fired within the hour."

"That's terrible. You should complain to the Human Rights Commission."

"I did—I wrote them a long letter. They wrote back that my dismissal was unfair and that I should get in touch with the Unemployment Board. The Board is paying me Unemployment Insurance till I find another job. But from what I get I couldn't buy myself a half-decent housecoat."

Her mentioning the housecoat reminded me of the dress I had forgotten to bring. I ran out without telling her where I was going, only begging her to keep the front door open as I should be back soon and would not like to be met by her husband again.

I drove at breakneck speed and returned with the dress and the pantyhose. On the way I threw out the cheap Army and Navy wrapper and put the stuff in a Bay Store plastic bag. After all, a thing should be judged by its worth and not by the store from which it is purchased.

Maura was delighted with the dress. It fitted her as if it had been made to measure. I walked around her several times, looking at her from various angles with the air of an experienced tailor. And I couldn't help congratulating myself on my excellent judgement. The sleeves could be shortened a couple of inches, and the hem could be raised by about the same length. Some letting out in the waist and the hips might be deemed necessary. Otherwise the dress fitted perfectly.

"This is beautiful,Tristan," she exclaimed."It's the best dress I've had for years."

"Try on the pantyhose," I said smugly. "If they don't fit I'll return them and get you another pair."

But all her mind was on the dress."I like this dress . . . it's gorgeous—it's fantastic," she kept repeating.

"You don't have to worry from this day on, Maura. All your troubles are over. I'll buy your groceries for you and when I get back on full salary I'll pay your rent as well."

"I don't want to burden you with the rent. He'll pay or I will take him to court. But I want something more important from you. Can you . . . ?"

"Anything."

"I want you to stand beside me—I want you to fight for the liberation of my sisters. I want you to fight against male chauvinism and for the equality of the sexes. Women everywhere have been trampled on by men—their individuality denied to them. They have no existence of their own; their sole purpose is to enrich men's lives. At best women are childbearers, but more often just sex objects. They are never treated as equals, and equality is what we seek as our birthright. Male supremacy has its origin in male tyranny, and we must fight this tyranny wherever we find it."

"How do I fight?" I asked, a bit confused.

She ignored my question and continued: "In this struggle we must enroll our black brethren. They, too, have been oppressed and exploited by white males. As an Indian, and a member of the oppressed races, you could become a rallying point for all those who wish to strike for freedom."

I didn't quite understand everything that Maura said, but I understood enough to realize that a grave injustice was being done to half the world's population and that the hour for battle had come. I could see myself with a banner at the head of a million women goose-stepping with babes in their arms and sanitary pads between their legs.

"I'll join you in the fight," I said.

Maura's eyes lit up with a newly found confidence. She took my hands in her own and said,"We'll make history, Tristan. Come, kiss me goodnight."

"Where should I kiss you?" I asked, wondering what part of her body she would offer me.

"Kiss me where you would kiss a brother or a sister."

As I did not have a brother or a sister, I didn't know where to kiss her. But she solved my dilemma by kissing me on the nose.

"It's not that I don't love you, Tristan.. But duty comes first," she cautioned.

5

Today is Sunday. I had resolved not to contact Maura until Monday, for I needed time to think things out. I also wanted to see if Maura would miss me and contact me on her own. Well, I have done all the thinking, and I have given Maura all the time in the world to contact me. To wait another day would be to waste another day. If Maura loses me, she has no one but herself to blame.

I phoned Maura. "I thought you would phone me," I said.

"I thought you'd phone me, Tristan."

"It's your turn," I tried to make light of the matter.

"No, it's yours. It's always for a man to phone a girl."

"Not if you believe in equality of the sexes!"

"Ah, but we don't have it yet. When we do, things will be different."

That sounded logical enough and I conceded her the argument. Besides, I had more important matters on my mind and I asked her to have supper with me at Sandra's. She agreed. I was to pick her up at seven: she would be watching out for my car from her window.

My quandary was how much of my past I should volunteer to Maura. Should I tell her everything about myself in one evening and thereby run the risk of losing her, or should I reveal my life in bits and pieces and spread it over several days? As I debated the issue, it became clear that in the end it would not matter how I went about my business. First or last, I would have to tell her the most fearful story of my life—my attempt at murder. This story apart, the rest might even do me credit. That I was born in India and was the only child of an Anglo-Indian nurse and a British pilot might give me oriental mystery with a bit of class. That I was educated at a modern high-rise university at Leeds and not some centuries old crumpled-down college makes me an up-to-date scholar. My passionate involvement with Heather is proof of my masculinity. My marriage to Elsa and the estrangement following the birth of a son is evidence that I am no old fossil but a man of the times. My affair with the beautiful Marie should make her jealous and expedite the consummation of our love. But how would I explain to Maura why I fired three shots at Marion—Marie's sister—after Marie deserted me? Would she understand that I fired the shots not to kill Marion but merely to destroy the womb: the source—as I saw it then—of all human suffering? Dr Enright understood and the judge understood and the jury understood that I was no common murderer, but that I rather thought of myself as a saviour. They, of course, pointed out to me the slight error in my comprehension of the world and my role in it. And later, during the two years I was in a hospital in Kamsack, the good doctor explained to me that if I was a true saviour, I should save the world through love and life, not hate and murder. I can still remember a nurse shaking her forefinger at me the day I was leaving the hospital and saying: "Go, Tristan, go and save the world. But no more fooling with the gun." And since then I have never touched a gun or thought of killing anybody—and only occasionally about killing myself.

Maura was waiting for me in the yellow dress I had presented her. As she got into the car she thanked me again and said how gorgeous it was. She asked me if she looked pretty in it, and I swore that I had not known a woman lovelier than she. This pleased her, though she complained that she had unusually thin arms and legs. "But, mind you," she said, "I wouldn't like breasts any bigger than what I have. I am a woman—not a sex object."

We got to Sandra's. It is right opposite the railway station and provides a magnificent view of the rolling stock. Before it became Sandra's, it was Doyle's, Fryer's, Roma's, Martha's and half a dozen others. Every owner of the restaurant lost money until Sandra came along. Sandra had ideas. She got two sets of bills printed: one in red and the other in blue. Red bills were presented to patrons who were single, separated or divorced, and they were entitled to a twenty percent discount on the total amount. Blue bills were for married couples only, and they got no discount. Both the singles and the marrieds flocked to Sandra's: the singles to take advantage of the discounts, the marrieds to assert that they would need more than a twenty percent discount before they parted from their loved ones. The singles formed a club known as the Red Billers, and the marrieds a club called the Blue Billers. Both groups flaunted their respective bills threateningly in each other's faces as they paid in cash to Sandra. There were some folks who kept alternating between red and blue bills. They did not make good customers and generally finished up in hospitals where, under the provincial health scheme, they got their meals free.

Luckily we didn't have to wait for long before we got a table to ourselves. But it was situated in the middle of the room and people were moving around all the time. A group sitting next to us was thumping the table and yelling and shouting. In such an atmosphere I could hardly tell my life story or expect Maura to respond to all its nuances. In addition, Maura was uncooperative: she gave all her attention to the T-bone steak she had ordered. The knife was blunt and I could appreciate her difficulties. I had ordered a mushroom omelette and had fewer problems.

When we were halfway through dinner, and the time for paying the bill came closer, I decided to get my money's worth. I had hoped Maura would ask me what was the business I wanted to discuss with her, but it seemed she had forgotten. And I didn't quite know where to begin. It would, of course, help if she were to ask me questions. And I began asking her just those questions I wanted her to ask me.

The first question I wanted to be asked was about my childhood. So I asked her about hers. She mistook my purpose and began narrating her childhood days with her brothers on a farm in Cut Knife. It was boring, and I put an end to it by asking her where she got her education. Instead of providing me an opportunity of discoursing on my Leeds' days, she began telling me everything about her school in Wilkie and the year she spent at my college in Erigon—as if that mattered. I next asked her when she got married. Once again she missed the clue, but thank God she was brief this time. She said she would rather not discuss unpleasant things on an evening such as this. "Fine with me," I said, turning round to order a bottle of Moose Jaw wine.

I saw Horace. He was walking with a scowl on his face towards the cashier. In one hand he had an extinguished pipe at which he kept pulling, in the other he held a blue bill high above his head to display it. His wife, cute as a gopher, stood waiting for him at the half-open door.

"Horace!" I cried out, quite forgetting that I was in a public place. He looked at me disapprovingly, and I quickly atoned for my indiscretion by shouting aloud, "Dr Peabody."

Horace shuffled up to our table, still holding the blue bill above his head. "Tristan, I am disappointed in you. Your conduct at the marathon shamed the fine institution of which, I presume, you are still a member."

I felt angry, but I didn't show it. He had no right to upbraid me in the presence of Maura. Besides, had he forgotten what he himself was doing there? I noticed that the middle finger of the hand he had had round the fat arse was in a splint. I wondered if she had chewed it up.

"I'm sorry, sir," I said, and went on to introduce Maura to him, "This is Maura Hawkins—my partner at the marathon."

He bowed gracefully from the waist and in the act dropped his goose-quill pen. I picked it up and put it behind his ear. This softened his attitude towards me and he said, "Come and see me in my office, Tristan, whenever you happen to be on

Campus."

"I'm going to be there tomorrow. I want to ask Dr Dunlop when i can resume teaching."

"Patrick Dunlop is no longer the Chairman."

"What?"

"Dunlop resigned last week, and I have been appointed acting Chairman by the Dean. There will be an election for a new Chairman in September."

"Will you be running, sir?"

"I don't want to, Tristan. I have my poetry to write. But immense pressure is being put on me by concerned members of the Department. I might have to forego my personal life for the good of the Department. Dunlop intends to stand again for the chairmanship!"

"Dr Dunlop! Why did he resign?"

"I wish I could answer that question; it has baffled everyone I have met. But I think I know why, and I shall tell you tomorrow. Dunlop's move is the most Machiavellian in the annals of Canadian history since Confederation."

"I can't believe it!"

He looked at me, smiled, tapped me on the back with his pipe, and ambled away. "Good night, sir," I called out after him, but he did not respond.

"Who's he?" asked Maura, after Peabody was out of sight.

"He is the Campus poet, celebrated throughout the province for his 'divorce poems.' He has been a great patron of mine and if he is elected Chairman I'll have no difficulty getting back to teaching and my full salary. And then I shall be able to pay your rent. I brought you here so that we could talk—there are things about me you should know. I want you to know now, so that you don't regret later."

"What is it that you want me to know," she asked, a little startled.

"You know I'm married."

"Yeah, you said so."

"And that I have a son."

"I didn't. Where is he?"

"I don't know."

"You don't know?"

"No. You see, I was sick—I was in hospital for two years. When I got back my lawyer told me that Elsa—that's my wife—had fled to Germany with my boy and that under no circumstances was I to contact them. In fact there was no way I could contact them; I didn't have their address."

"Do you pay her support money?"

"Do I? Four hundred a month! A cool four hundred hard-earned dollars are deducted at the source from what I get as salary continuance insurance and sent directly to her. And to top it all, the salary continuance insurance is a mere seventy percent of my regular pay."

"Seventy percent, you said!"

"It used to be sixty. But the Government got scared that we folks on salary continuance might form a union and demand eighty percent. So they offered us seventy. We should never have accepted it—we would have made the largest and most powerful union in Canada."

"Hum! Do you love your boy?"

"I do now, but I didn't when we were together."

"How come?"

I told Maura that I married Elsa on the rebound, after I had been cheated by a promiscuous girl called Heather. I didn't love Elsa, but I thought that marriage with a steady girl would bring some stability into my life. It didn't. I started hating everything about Elsa, including my son. But what I found most offensive was her weight: 180 pounds, with or without the baby.

"So that's why you like me—because I'm thin."

I ignored the remark. I told her that my loathing for Elsa reached a point where I could not bear the sight of her. The loss of vision in one eye made me determined to kill myself, and I rented for the purpose a farmhouse in Corwind (the one where the marathon took place). But I was saved by the timely appearance of Marie, a grocer's daughter who convinced me that I had much to live for and much to give to the world. I believed her, but when she deserted me I did something which—which I wouldn't do now. And I paused for her to ask me what I had done. Instead she asked:

"Was Marie pretty?"

"She was very pretty."

"Prettier than I am?"

"She was different, but that's not important. What happened then was that I . . ."

"Oh, Tristan," she interrupted. "I don't like to think that she was prettier than me."

"Forget it," I said impatiently. "You know what I did?"

"You tried to kill yourself for her?"

"No! I tried to kill her twin sister, Marion, who looked exactly like her."

"Oh."

"I fired three shots at her. But I didn't really mean to kill her. I only wanted to destroy the womb so that there would be no more misery in the world."

"Did you kill her?"

"No, I missed."

"I wish you hadn't."

"Why?"

"Because she must be as beautiful as her sister! You said they looked exactly alike."

"Is that all you can think?"

"What do you want me to say?"

"Are you not afraid of me? Are you not . . . ?"

"No. Why should I be? You didn't kill her!"

"But I tried!"

"So what, Tristan? You tried and failed! The proof is in the pudding. If you didn't kill her—you're innocent."

"You may be right there," I said. "They didn't hang me—they only charged me with attempted manslaughter."

"Manslaughter? It was a woman you tried to kill!"

"Sure, but the police called it manslaughter."

"They did! The bastards! We women don't exist. Even if you kill one of us it's manslaughter. Tristan, we have a long fight ahead of us with these male chauvinist pigs."

"Yes, but don't you want to know what happened to me?"

"Go on."

"Dr Enright testified in court that I wasn't a murderer and two other psychiatrists agreed with him. The court ruled that I wasn't to possess firearms and that I should be admitted to a hospital for observation."

"I'm told that the hospital food is very bland. What did they give you for dinner?"

"Look, Maura, let me get through this quickly."

"What! Is there something more?"

"At Kamsack the good doctors told me that if I was to save the world, I should do it through love and kindness—not with a gun."

"I don't agree with the doctors," said Maura, wiping her mouth with a napkin. "It's all very good to talk about love, but there are some who can only be reformed by a shotgun. Do you think you could change Ralph with love? Or that policeman of yours who would deny us our identity?"

I gave up. It was close to eleven when I suggested to Maura we should go to my place for a quick drink. She agreed, and then changed her mind. She said it was getting late for the babysitter and I should take her home.

6

Today I paid my first visit to the college in six months. Nothing had changed there except that the administrative building, which houses the History Department, has been renamed Templum Scientiae. In the centre of the building there is a huge pit, and around it are situated the business offices, classrooms and faculty offices. All the inside offices overlooking the pit have glass walls, and I have spent many pleasant hours sitting in my office and watching the extracurricular activities for which the place is justly renowned. This morning the whole building was resounding with Ed Landy's Jazz Band, but I was too preoccupied to tap my feet.

To see the Chairman, one has to pass through the secretary's office. Miss Brenda Mortimer, the Department secretary, was typing when I knocked on the door. "Good morning," I called out breezily but lost courage when she turned half-round to face me and said "Yes." She has enormous breasts which she supports by resting them against the edge of her desk. It is her breasts, I think, which keep most of the students and faculty at bay.

"I'd like to see Dr Peabody," I muttered.

"Dr Peabody is busy. Do you have an appointment with him?"

"He asked me to see him."

"When?"

"He said I could drop in any time."

"It will be another half hour. Would you wait in room 415

and check with me around 10.30."

"Room 415? That's my office!"

"It's the graduate coffee lounge."

"My office has been turned into a coffee lounge! Who the hell did that?"

She looked at me with disgust, took a half turn on her swivel chair and resumed typing.

"There are no graduate students in this Department," I added.

"We know that," she retorted smugly. "We are trying to build a graduate department, and we are trying to make this place attractive so that students will come."

"Attractive—my ass!" I shouted, losing all control of myself. Peabody must have heard me, for he called out from the inner office, "Brenda, send him in."

I stormed into Peabody's office. He was standing behind his huge new desk. He was wearing his doctoral gown of many colours as was his habit when writing poetry. But today, for the first time, I saw him sporting a mortarboard as well. It had a maple leaf painted on the top, and there was a long tassel which fell over his left ear.

"What is this I hear—my office turned into a bloody students' lounge?"

"Tristan, Tristan," he pronounced my name gravely, and in a deep guttural voice. And while he did so, he looked me straight in the eyes. I returned the stare and would have outstared him. But I had never been faced with a mortarboard before and I was soon intimidated.

"I'm sorry, sir," I apologized.

"Your office was turned into a coffee lounge by Dunlop. It was one of his last acts before he resigned."

"Is he trying to get rid of me, sir?"

"I will not impute motives to my colleagues. It is for you to draw your own conclusions."

"I'll ask him."

"And make matters worse for yourself! You may find comfort

in this, Tristan, that you are not his only victim. The Department is in a shambles and I don't even know where to begin."

"Sir, I want to get back to teaching. I'm finding it very difficult to make ends meet on what I get as salary continuance. I am going to have additional responsibilities. I'm all right now. You can ask my doctor—he will certify that I am no longer sick."

"We don't need to ask your doctor. We can judge things for ourselves. The first sign of health and sanity, Tristan, is loyalty to your department. And every loyal member will tell you of the harm Dunlop has done."

"I've always been a loyal member," I vouched.

"I believe you. But unfortunately your loyalty has only earned you grief. If I am elected Chairman—God forbid, I have my poetry to write—I shall see that your services to the Department are suitably rewarded. I have always had a tender spot for you, you know."

Peabody went on to explain to me the politics of the Department, and I must say I was greatly impressed by his astuteness and how well he had figured out the crafty Dunlop. Dunlop wanted another three-year term as Chairman, but he had so mismanaged the affairs of the Department that his chances of being reelected were exceedingly slim. Therefore he devised this brilliant strategy: he resigned four months before his term expired. The person appointed as Acting Chairman would now have the arduous task of creating order from the disorder he inherited from Dunlop. He would have to rid the Department of mendacity, evasion, dishonesty, hypocrisy, pretence, perjury and jesuitry. In the process of discharging his duties, he would himself become unpopular and thereby enhance Dunlop's chances of being reelected. The problem as Peabody saw it was to rescue the Department from the evils that Dunlop had introduced during his reign and still be elected Chairman. This was no easy task, and I promised him my unequivocal support.

"At present there are twelve voting members in the Department, including Dunlop and myself. We both, of course, will vote for ourselves. But the voting will end up in a tie. That will give the Dean a vote to break the tie, and you know, Tristan, to whom his vote will go. He will give it to Dunlop. They are both British, and you know how clannish the British are. It was not for nothing that they ruled half the world."

I didn't like Peabody attacking the British, perhaps because I had a British father. But I saw that at such a time truth was more important than personal sentiments.

"I need your vote to break the tie," Peabody continued. "And if you can resume your duties you can vote."

"You have my vote, sir."

"It's not I who need your vote. The Department needs your vote—your vote will decide whether there will be a History Department in this college or not."

"There will always be a History Department," I asserted, raising a clenched fist above my head.

"Well said, Tristan," chuckled Peabody. "I will have a word about you with the Dean. You may go now."

As I was walking out elated with myself, Peabody called out, "Come and see me whenever you want, but remember to make an appointment with Miss Mortimer. She doesn't approve of my seeing anyone without an appointment."

"Thank you, sir," I said. And I ran straight to my car to carry the good news to Maura. I thought I could stop on the way at the bank and ask for a small loan to pay her rent.

I was turning on the ignition when I heard a tap on the window of the passenger side. It was the spindly Dunlop with his grimy eyes and pointed beard. I rolled down the window and told him that I was in a bit of a rush—I had to get somewhere. He laughed and asked me to open the door, which I did. He got in and sat down beside me.

"Now that I'm not the Chairman, you can afford to be in a bit of a rush!"

I didn't know what to say. He was right; had he still been

Chairman I would have treated him differently. But I knew why I was being surly.

"Why did you turn my office into a graduate lounge?"

"If we hadn't turned it into something or the other, we would have lost it. Space is at premium here."

"But there are no graduate students!"

"That's exactly why I turned it into a graduate lounge. You could have your office back whenever you resumed teaching."

This thought had never occurred to me. Dunlop was crafty all right, but he wasn't using his cunning against me. He had devised a way of keeping my office for me. But I would need to know more about the game he was up to.

"Why did you resign from the Chairmanship?"

"I am going in for a kidney operation next week. And after that I go with my family to Europe for three months' convalescence. I hope you don't begrudge me that!"

"No, I don't. But . . . you do intend to stand for the Chairmanship again?"

"Not if I can help it, Tristan. I have my editing to do. But immense pressure is being put upon me by concerned members of the Department."

I was surprised that both he and Peabody spoke in identical words when they were asked if they would stand for the Chairmanship. Was the phrase "immense pressure is being put upon me by concerned members" a magic formula every prospective candidate had to repeat? Were the words as firmly established or as unalterable as "God Save the Queen" or "Thy Will Be Done"?

"Sir, may I ask a question that concerns me deeply?"

"You have already assumed the role of the inquisitor. But I wish you'd stop calling me 'sir'."

"When can I go back to teaching?"

"That will depend on your doctor."

"Oh!"

"If your doctor thinks you are fit to teach, you could start in September."

"You mean I'll have to sit still for four months before I can draw my full salary?"

"I would think so. The semester is just over and classes don't begin till fall. The college will do all it can to save every cent of your salary."

"I don't agree with you. I think I'll be back on full pay very soon."

"What makes you think so?"

"I've just seen the Acting Chairman, and he is going to speak to the Dean about me."

"Ah! That explains why you were in such a hurry when you saw me. What price did Peabody ask?"

"Dr Peabody asks for nothing but loyalty to the Department."

"Hum. How do you demonstrate that loyalty? By voting for him, Tristan?"

I did not reply. My fear was that if he found out I had promised my vote to Peabody, he would be my enemy for life. And if he won the election, he would make sure I remained on salary continuance as long as I lived.

"Well, anyway, that gives Peabody two votes: his own and yours," Dunlop mused.

"What do you mean? He already has six votes and needs one more to break the tie."

"Six votes? Do you think the entire Department is as crazy as you are?" And getting out of my car he added, "He'll probably get only one vote—his own."

"You mean I'll remain on salary continuance?"

"Until the term begins."

"You'll oppose me?"

"No, Tristan. If I started opposing every fool I came across, I wouldn't last a day. I hired you. It was a bloody mistake, but we must learn to live with our mistakes."

"Thank you," I said, and drove off. I didn't go to the bank—I went straight to the liquor store. I bought a bottle of scotch and drank and drank till I fell asleep. I had a most beautiful dream. I dreamt that I was the Chairman and Maura my secretary. We were lying beside each other on a couch, kissing quick kisses. Nearby sat Clare on her potty, repeating rhythmically: "Dada . . . Mama . . . Dada . . . Mama . . ."

7

When I told Maura that I wouldn't be able to pay her rent until September, her lovely face fell. But brave and noble as she is, she asked me not to fret—said that woman does not live by bread alone. I assured her that we would never be short of bread, that when it came to the crunch I was worth $90,000. She was overjoyed and wanted to know why I hadn't told her this before.

"Because I still have to get the money," I said.

"Where is it?"

"With Sun Life. I have an insurance policy of $90,000. The company is doing its best to wriggle out of the deal since they know that I am no coward. But I've got them by the balls, and I'm going to pay my dues until the day I die."

"Oh!" she sighed, losing colour.

"Don't worry, my darling. I'm not going to die. You go now and get the grocery list ready."

Maura began getting a list of the things she needed, while I squatted opposite Clare. She, as usual, was seated on her potty. She is always on her potty, not simply because she is constipated and continually making tee-tee (which is, Maura tells me, the liberated word for wee-wee), but because it is the only thing that goes with her size. It was designed and made by her carpenter father and given to her on her first birthday, which was some three weeks ago. It is quite an ingenious contraption: by merely folding and rearranging its various components it can be turned into a chair, a table, a recliner and a toboggan. She has taken to it as a fish takes to water, and I don't see why Maura bothers to strap her to it.

Clare sat with her right fist in her mouth, studying me with her large, blue eyes. She was a picture of calm and serenity, outdoing Diogenes himself in his wooden tub. No wonder that early in his life Wordsworth described the child as "Mighty prophet! seer blest!" and then lived to a ripe old age writing abominable poetry to prove to all "That there hath passed away a glory from the earth." I felt I was in the presence of a mighty soul. I fell prostrate at her feet and touched them to my forehead. She accepted the homage like a pontiff, tapping me several times on the head with her left hand. Just then Maura called out, "What the hell are you doing?" Absorbed as I was in higher pursuits, I told her to mind her own business. I had spoken without thinking. I looked up and saw her take a deep breath in preparation for one of her deafening screams. I rushed to her and threw my arms around her and pressed my lips to hers. Slowly she breathed out, and I could see from the volume what an explosion I had averted with my presence of mind.

The list Maura gave me wasn't long, but it had things on it I had never heard before—things like abalone, succotash, kumquats, zucchini, prosciutto and calamari. The shop assistants sent me wheeling my grocery cart forwards and backwards through every aisle in the store. I was quite happy, though, for it made me feel like a responsible family man and I could look the fat housewives in the face. But when I finished shopping, I saw that all I had bought could be got into one large paper bag. Hardly an image befitting a man on the threshold of a new life! So I bought two hundred-pound bags of Windsor Crystal salt.

As the trunk of my car does not open, I put the bags of salt on the hood. It was amazing to see how all the strange noises that came from under the hood disappeared and I could once again hear—as I did when I first bought the car—the gentle purring of the engine. In fact the car ran so smoothly that I twice got down to check the number plates and make sure I wasn't driving away somebody else's vehicle.

Maura said I had a shopper's eye, but that the salt was a waste as there was no water softener in the house. She asked me to go and return it. I said I would rather keep it; it would save me the expense of buying another car when the time came. But the salt was gone in the morning, and I had much trouble getting the police to make a note of the theft.

As we agreed to share the household work, I said I'd do the cooking and she should do the washing. But she insisted on doing the cooking, arguing that she had a meeting to attend at eight and wouldn't have time to do the washing. I was about to suggest that we toss a coin and leave the decision to Providence when she asked if I would baby-sit as well.

"Gladly," I assured her.

"I'll be back by eleven," she said.

"No need to rush. Take your time," I answered.

She gave me a look full of exasperation and then shook her head from side to side. She often does that.

Maura cooked an Italian dinner—spaghetti with marinara sauce. It tasted delicious after I had sprinkled it with pepper and seasoning salts. I congratulated her on her expertise, and she took my hand and pulled it under the table and squeezed it. Just then a car screeched to a stop in front of the house and honked several times. As Maura ran out, I peeped through the window. It was a battered red van with several women in it—shouting, gesticulating. The van was covered with words crudely painted in black, of which I could read only a few. They were SKAM, WOOW, FAW, SOL and WITCH.

After Maura had left, I took Clare off the potty and put her on the floor. I tried to make her walk, but she couldn't without my help. But she could crawl on her own, with her legs straight and her rear end high in the air. I'd go to one side of the room and clap my hands. And she would come crawling to me. I'd go to another part of the room and clap my hands. And she'd come crawling there. Soon I too began to crawl, imitating her as well as I could. She didn't take any notice of that, but her father Ralph did. He had come down to see his girlfriend off. He began laughing the way he did when I first saw him. But this time he sobered up to speak a few words:

"Hey, where do you come from?"

"India."

"India? What brought you to this goddamn place?"

"I don't know."

"I bet you don't," he avowed, going up the stairs.

I wish he hadn't spoken to me. I thought of his words and felt frightened and lonely. Had I indeed lost my way? What was I doing here with another man's wife, another man's child? Memories of my past stormed my mind in a terrifying bid to scare me. But I brushed them aside. I had not lost my way. I had taken a road. That road led to another, and that to yet another. And wherever I might now be, I was a step closer to heaven than I was before. Clare and I, even with our rear ends sticking in the air, would grace God's presence one day, while he—he will never go higher than the stairs he descends to mock me.

Ralph had put an end to our game. Anyway, it was time for Clare to go to bed. I picked her up and put her on the potty for the tee-tee. To assist the process, I said "Hush, hush . . ." as I had seen Elsa do to our boy. But Clare sat immobile and the pot stayed dry. Something was wrong—"hush" wasn't the right word. Then the magic word flashed on my mind. I filled my lungs with air, and emptied them slowly to the sound of "shoo." I did it several times, and I could hear the tee-tee trickling into the pot. After the performance, I laid Clare on the bed and sat down beside her. She wore the expression of a person trying to recognize me—the sort of expression which seems to say: "I've seen you before!"

As I can't sing a lullaby, I thought of telling Clare the story of the creation. And I told it in baby language. Before the beginning there was only God and nothing else. God felt like doing something. So the first day He said, "Let there be light." And by golly, there was light. He could hardly believe his eyes. Then followed a week of making, such a week as God had not known before. He made the earth, the sky, the water, and filled them with all the animals and birds and fishes he could think of. It was a lot of hard work and took God full five days. But He was sort of getting bored, when on the sixth day He had a bright idea. He said: "Let us make man in our image, after our likeness." So He picked up some dirt and made the first man and put life into him. He shouldn't have done it, but there's no stopping God. On the seventh day He threw up His arms and said, "So what?" and flopped into his chair. And I fell gently athwart Clare and kissed her. She smiled and muttered, "Dada. . . Papa . . . Papa . . . "

It wasn't long before she began crying. I felt her diaper but it was dry. She must have been hungry, the poor kid, and so I went to the fridge and got her the bottle. She sucked at it half-heartedly and then pushed it away and vomited. I wiped the rancid, curdlike substance from around her mouth and chin with the bottom edge of my shirt. I gave her the bottle again, but she positively refused to take it. What she wanted was not milk, but human kindness. I applied some of the marinara sauce that Maura had made to my nipple, sprinkled salt and pepper on it, and put it in her mouth. She is, in the words of the learned Dr Spock, an "eager beaver." She took not only my nipple but the entire areola into her mouth and sucked and sucked till she fell asleep. When I pulled the nipple out, I found it red and sore. But it stood erect and wasn't retracted like the other one. If only I could persuade Maura to breast-feed the baby, her nipples too would become firm like mine. However, it wasn't her breasts or my own that I was thinking about, rather the enlightenment that had come to me. I had learnt that what a child needs is not milk but love; that though there is a substitute for mother's milk, there is no substitute for the human breast.

It was close to midnight when Maura returned. I was lying awake on her bed, thinking what I could do to bring some joy and happiness into Clare's life. I thought of my own frightened childhood after my father's death and the terrible fear that my mother might leave me and go away with another man. I thought of my boy who would be three now and how fat Elsa had deprived him of a father's loving care. And I thought of the millions of children in the world who had never known parental love and who must grow up to hate and despise everything around them. Surely, surely something could be done.

Maura came in very excited. She switched on the lights and took of her clothes and threw them at me and laughed. She jumped on me and kissed me all over the face and said that I was a darling and that her comrades approved of me.

"What comrades?" I asked.

"Our sisters in the Movement. They thought you were a dear when I told them that you bought the groceries, washed the dishes and baby-sat for me. They respect you for being an Indian. Vanessa said you come from an ancient civilization where women are given a place of pride. You had a woman Prime Minister?"

"Who's Vanessa?"

"She is the commander of SKAM. She wants to appoint you as her deputy."

"SKAM?"

"Yes, S-K-A-M—Society for Killing All Men. It is our militant arm, our nuclear force which we'll use only in the last resort. It will lead to the extermination of the Western man."

"I don't want to have anything to do with it. I only want to love you and Clare."

"You can't love me and not my principles. Love and duty go together."

"Couldn't we have love first?" I asked, unzipping my trousers.

"You are cunning, Tristan. But I love you, I love you, I love you."

She got me to lie on my back with my arms at my sides and my legs stretched straight. She climbed on top of me and, pressing down on me, began to move her hips in a circular motion. I could feel my penis hardening against her belly, but I couldn't get it into her. I asked if it wouldn't be better if she were to lie on her back and I on her.

"No."

By now I had a full erection and her movements were hurting me.

"Can't we try some other posture?"

"No. I get a better orgasm this way."

"But what about me?"

"Shh, be quiet," she admonished, now working her hips in a frenzy.

Maura gasped, shuddered, moaned and made weird noises. I could see her coming to a climax. Just then there was the blare of the saxophone. She bounced off me like a rubber ball, picked up a shoe and hurled it at the ceiling. "Stop it—you prick," she yelled.

The sound of the saxophone died and with it Maura's spirit. She returned dejected to the bed and lay down beside me. She put her arms around me and began to sob. Between sobs, she spoke: "I don't want anything . . . I only want to be loved. I don't want to fight men . . . I don't care what happens to other women. I am so unhappy. I only want . . . "

I rubbed my cheek against her tears. I asked her if she would like to be a flower girl.

"What's that?"

"Get me a lipstick."

She went into the bathroom and got me four lipsticks. She wasn't crying any more; like a child she seemed to have forgotten her immediate sorrow and was now interested in the newest toy.

I got her to lie down. Applying the lipstick generously to my lips, I printed small close kisses on every inch of her body. When I had finished, I asked her to go up to the wardrobe mirror and admire my handiwork. She was fascinated as she viewed herself from different angles and positions. She complained that there were fewer flowers on one buttock than on the other. I counted them; she was right. I planted four more kisses on the buttock. This delighted her, and she strode up and down the room as though she were a contestant in a Beauty Queen competition.

When I stood up to leave, she flung her arms around my neck and, heaving herself up, encircled my waist with her legs. She kissed me vehemently. But the next morning she phoned up to call me a son of a bitch. One of her "sisters" was coming to see her and the flowers wouldn't wash off.

8

Life has fallen into a pattern, and I'm happier than I have been for a long time. Most nights I sleep in my own apartment, but by midday I am at Maura's place to share the household work. I give her a hand with the gardening if Ralph is not around—I can't get to like him and I dread his laughter. But as a rule I work inside the house, and there is always a lot to do. There's the usual dusting and vacuuming to be done, clothes to be washed, Clare's tee-tee to be swabbed and her pot to be cleaned. I have to go and buy the groceries, peel the potatoes, chop the onions, throw the garbage out. As Maura doesn't like my cooking, it means that washing dishes has become exclusively my chore. Though she agrees in principle that I am entitled to my turn at cooking, she feels that by aptitude and skill I am better at washing and should stick to it. For about an hour every afternoon I take Clare out to give her mother time to read, and to write letters. As there is no stroller in the house, I have to carry her in my arms. It's a shame her father didn't think of adding wheels to the potty. In the evenings Maura and I watch TV unless she has a meeting to attend. Once in a while we get a baby-sitter and dine out at Sandra's. Before I get back to my apartment for the night, I might kiss Maura from toe to head (as I did at the marathon), but I no longer take the bypass. And if Maura wants, we make love.

Maura seldom has an orgasm, and I think it has much to do with the posture she prefers. It is called "Riding St. George." I find it uncomfortable, but it is a posture that gives her complete control over the situation. I lie on my back with the soles of my feet touching each other. She sits on me as though she were on horseback, facing me, with her hands on my biceps. As she rides me she often kisses me, leans forwards and backwards; sometimes she turns round and faces the other way. She goes through various motions: starting with a trot, followed by a canter or a gallop and back to a trot again. While galloping she may ask me to touch her on the clitoris. I don't like doing it, for many a time she has given a whooping cry and fallen off the bed.

The one discordant note in our sexual life is Ralph. He has the uncanny knack of blowing the saxophone just when Maura is on the gallop. And the way Maura jumps makes me fear that one day she'll go through the roof. I have begged her to ignore him, and she agrees that that's what she ought to do. But at the first blast of the saxophone she forgets her resolution. I have to be on constant alert while she is making love; at the least sound I hold her down firmly with one hand and with the other cover her mouth. I do so, of course, with Maura's consent, for no one dare stop Maura from screaming against her wishes.

We generally get into an argument after we've made love. Today as Maura dismounted, she rebuked me for breast-feeding Clare, saying Clare would want the same from her and she didn't have any milk in her breasts.

"Nor do I," I said to comfort her.

"Then what is the point of breast-feeding?" she demanded.

"A big advantage is that the milk is always pure and the baby can't catch any intestinal infection from it. The mother's antibodies to diseases such as cold and measles and . . ."

"But you don't have any milk. You . . ."

"Hold on, will you, till I finish. The greatest single argument in favour of breast-feeding is that it creates an emotional tie between mother and child for which there is no substitute in my experience. It satisfies the child's natural instinct to suck, and sucking is the only instinct with which we are born. The more you get to suck as a baby, the more of a sucker you will be when you grow up, and one day you might rise to the top in this work-a-day world."

"Were you breast-fed?"

"Of course not! Can't you see that? If I were I'd be the Chairman by now. I know what I've lost, and I want Clare, and every baby in the world, breast-fed."

"I think you're crazy."

"If to generate love and bring happiness to little children is crazy, then I'm proud to be crazy."

Seeing that I was adamant on breast-feeding and nothing could change my mind about it, she turned to another subject to berate me. She objected to my telling Clare the story of creation and strictly forbade me to tell her how God created woman. She called the Bible a fairy tale written by a bunch of male chauvinists to subjugate women.

"Why should God create Eve from one of Adam's ribs when there was so much mud around?" she asked triumphantly.

"How do I know," I answered back. "He probably did not want to dirty his hands again."

"Was there a lack of water in the Garden of Eden?"

"No, but there might have been no soap."

Mine was an irreverent quip, and as a believer in the Bible I was regretting it when I saw Maura pondering over my remark. She bit her lower lip, and then spoke to me slowly and thoughtfully:

"I don't think you are right, Tristan; I don't agree that God created man first. It doesn't make sense. Why should He create man first when man thereafter must be born of woman. Why would God put the cart before the horse? No, God made woman first, but man made the myth that woman was created out of Adam's rib so that he could boss her."

"If this is so, why doesn't somebody refute the Bible?"

"We are trying to, but in the Catholic Church we have a cunning enemy."

"Don't be silly. You are forgetting the Church's glorification of Mary—the Mother of God."

"You mean Mary, the carpenter's wife?"

"That's blasphemy, Maura. What you say is a sin against the Holy Ghost."

"I hope it is—I hope it is the biggest sin of all. And I'll ask for no absolution either. I am going to confess to no man priest. Tell me, why don't we have women priests? Isn't the exclusion of women from priesthood a slap in our face? What right has an all-male hierarchy to rule over the lives of millions of women? Don't sit there dumb. Answer me, you Son of God!"

I was stumped. I had no argument with which to refute her. I closed my eyes and looked up to heaven for an answer, but none was forthcoming. I opened my eyes and looked down, and my full gaze fell on Maura's moist vagina. I thrust my head between her thighs and kissed it and kissed it and kissed it.

"Stop it. Answer my question," she said.

"I will. If the church allowed pretty women like you into the priesthood, with what mouth would we men confess our sins?"

That tickled her vanity, and she spoke with a smile at the corner of her lips. "So you agree that an injustice has been done to us."

"No. A terrible injustice has been done to man. God has made us so dependent on women."

"Vanessa is right—you men have pussy-envy."

"Don't bracket me with other men. What do I care what the others have. To me there is nothing more beautiful than you. How I wish that with every kiss I could put a child in your womb."

"Wouldn't that be nice, Tristan. I want to have a million children."

"And I would breast feed them all," I said.

Maura laughed, put her head on my chest and closed her eyes. I assumed she had fallen asleep, and I was scheming how best I could slip a pillow under her head and get away without waking her when she opened her eyes and sat bolt upright. There wasn't a trace of sleep in her eyes.

"Tristan, does your religion discriminate against women?"

"My religion! What's happened to you, Maura? What's my religion?"

"I always think of you as a Hindi."

"You mean a Hindu?"

"What's the difference?"

"Hindi is a language while Hindu is a race."

"Ah, I see. Well, then, a Hindu."

"I am no bloody Hindu," I protested.

"What does the Hindu religion say about women? Do they have women priests?"

"No, but they have female Goddesses."

"Do men worship these Goddesses?"

"You bet, unless they want their limbs racked and their heads chopped off."

"Tristan, this is news to me. Tell me more about these Goddesses. How many of them are there?"

"Two, that I've heard of, though there may be more. One is Kali, the Black Goddess, who wears a necklace made of human skulls. She has four hands. In two hands she holds a sword and a dagger, and in the other two severed heads with blood dripping from them. She has a long tongue which hangs from her wide mouth, and blood trickles down her chin and neck as she gorges on human flesh. Today things aren't too prosperous with this Goddess, for the law does not allow her anything more exotic than goat's blood."

"My God! What's the other like?"

"She is called Durga. With ten arms, she is prettier than Kali, but equally bloodthirsty. She is encircled with snakes and is always shown riding a lion. She slays demons and drinks their blood. Her biggest victory was over the buffalo demon, Mahisha, who could not be killed by either man or beast. Durga being neither man (but a woman) nor beast (but divine) slew the monster and drained his body of every drop of blood."

"Tristan, you stay here tonight."

I looked up. Maura was staring at me with her mouth half

open.

"Maura! You are not afraid?"

"I am."

"These Goddesses live in India."

"They could come here, couldn't they?"

"For what? What would they do in a cold country like this?"

"You came to Canada."

"Yes, but I had an MA from Leeds and I needed a job. These Goddesses are self-employed; besides they are tropical."

I went on to explain to Maura that Kali and Durga hunt only men, and that they never cross the high seas; and that though there might be a shortage of rice and lentils in India, there is no shortage of flesh.

Maura sat pensive for a while, then exclaimed: "We've been looking for a symbol for our banner. We could use one of the Goddesses. Which would you prefer?"

"I think Kali is better. She'll scare the men away."

"That she would, but the other has ten arms. And each arm could symbolize one of the attributes of our Movement."

"In that case have Durga."

"I should phone Vanessa and ask her."

Maura picked up the phone, and dialed. The number was engaged. She tried again, the number was still busy. She cursed Vanessa, calling her a bitch that barks at men during the day and has a long tête-á-tête with them on the phone at night. After half an hour of trying, she finally got Vanessa.

"Vanessa, I've just found the right symbol for our banner. I'm so excited, I couldn't wait till the morning . . .What?. . . 2 a.m.? You must be kidding!"

I looked at my watch. It was past two. I slipped away quietly, for I had an appointment with Clifford Enright at 9 a.m.

9

Enright was distracted and impatient when I saw him. He had broken his right arm, which was in plaster; he had misplaced his bifocals and couldn't find them; he had to catch a plane for Vancouver at 10.30 to attend a crash course in psychotherapy. He had little time for me, and in one way perhaps it was all for the best. He asked me what the matter was. I did not reply, but took off my shirt and vest and with the index fingers of both hands pointed at my nipples.

"The left looks a bit sore," he said, bringing his face close and squinting his eyes. With his fingers he pressed round the areola to see if there was any pus in it. "We'll get you to see a GP," he said.

"What for?"

"I don't know what this is due to. I have occasionally seen mothers with sore breasts, but obviously . . ."

"I've been breast feeding Clare," I said firmly in a bid to overpower him, and then sat back resignedly for the usual reactions I get from him every time I open my mouth. But for once he did not say, "Now, Tristan, do you think you are doing the right thing?" or "This is most unusual . . . I have never heard of such a thing before." Instead, he merely asked me to use a breast shield. I didn't know what a breast shield was, so he pulled out a manual and showed me a drawing of one. It consisted of a conical piece of clear plastic with a rubber nipple attached to its apex. The plastic is meant to fit snugly around the nipple.

"Anything else?" he asked.

"Yes. I think I'm all right now and would like to resume teaching. I need a fitness certificate from you."

"Could we leave this business for a few weeks?"

"You think I'm sick."

"No, I think nothing of the kind. But we could wait for a while. Anything else?"

"I want a baby from Maura."

"I see."

"I can't make her pregnant. Can you suggest what I should do? Do you have any pills that might work?"

"No, Tristan, I don't have any pills."

"What am I supposed to do?"

"Keep trying."

"For how long?"

"As long as it's necessary."

"Doctor, you're not being very helpful."

"I have two other patients to see before I catch my plane. So we could leave your problems till I get back. There is nothing wrong with your breasts. Clare is perhaps teething and has a few bites at your nipples. This is quite normal. Apply some cold cream and give your breasts a little rest. But if you must feed her, use the breast shield. She might prefer the breast shield, since your nipples are small—I mean they are not exactly designed for feeding . . . "

"All right," I said, and walked out. This was the first time I didn't thank him, nor did I wish him a pleasant trip. He had treated me with an abruptness befitting a pensioner in a charity hospital, hardly as a professor who is also a taxpayer. I was a victim of state medicare, where the doctor gets his fee and the patient the short end of the stick.

On my way to Maura's I stopped at the drug store and bought a breast shield. When I reached her place, Ralph was sitting on the front steps with Clare on his knees. I was about to turn around and leave when he stood up and stretched out his hand for me to shake. He didn't laugh while we shook hands, but there was a mischievous glint in his eyes.

"Welcome Tristan," he said with a bow. "Would you like tea or coffee?"

"Nothing. Where's Maura?"

"Ran out—down that road. Asked me to make you comfortable till she got back. Tea or coffee?"

"I'll come back later."

Just then Clare smiled at me and said, "Papa. . . Papa."

"See! That's a clever kid—knows her Papa. I'm only her Dada," said Ralph.

"Clare doesn't know the difference," I remarked, and turned to leave.

He suddenly thrust Clare into my arms. He said he had something important to talk to me about—had been waiting for an opportunity like this one for a long time. There was nothing I could do but submit. I had my chance to run away when I first saw him, but I had missed it.

"Well, what is it?" I asked.

"Please stop fucking my wife," he said.

"What?"

"I beg you not to fuck my wife. She is my wife—we were joined in holy matrimony by Reverend Alwyn Cosbey in St. Marks Chapel."

"I'm sorry, but I don't understand."

"Please," he said in a piteous voice.

"There's some misunderstanding," I said with assumed dignity.

"Misunderstanding?" And he burst into laughter. "Good guns! I've seen it with my own two eyes, and I didn't know whether to laugh or weep as she rode you." And he went and sat astride a lawn chair and began riding it as if it were a horse, uttering sounds of hoofbeats and swaying his body forwards and backwards.

"What evidence do you have that I am having sex with Maura?" I asked.

"Evidence! What's evidence?"

"Proof."

"Ah," he exclaimed, getting off the chair. And with a toss of his head, "Come with me—I'll show you something."

I climbed the stairs after him, carrying Clare in my arms. We came to the bedroom which was small and dirty and smelled of urine. There was no furniture in it except a large bed on which lay a saxophone. On the floor there was a huge pile of clothes: shirts, jeans, cardigans, vests, towels and sheets. He kicked the clothes away and asked me what I could see on the floor.

"Nothing," I replied.

"Look carefully. Can't you see something where my big toe is?" And he moved a leg forward.

"I see a hole."

"Now bend your ass and look through the hole."

I gave Clare to him and did as he asked me. But I could see nothing.

"I see nothing," I said.

"Don't be so fuckin' blind. Look again."

I did. I saw Maura's bed. The hole was right over the bed. When I put my eye to it and peered I could see the bed.

"I see," I said.

"What do you see? You see none of the fuckin' thing I have to see every night. God help me! When I first came to this house and I was told you were an Indian, I thought I'd learn some grand sexual poses from you. I said to myself, 'Now here's a guy from the land of the *Kamasutra*. He will teach us the art of sex—the sixty-four ways to fuck a woman.' But what did I see? I saw her riding you like you would ride a donkey. There were days I almost wept for you. And when I couldn't take it any longer I'd blow that bloody thing there." And he pointed to the saxophone.

"I'm going to tell Maura about this," I said swallowing my spittle so as not to explode.

"You will not."

"I will."

"You'll be a dead man."

"I don't care. What do you expect me to do, you bastard?"

"I want you to throw her off once in a while and show us one of your Indian tricks."

"You are a pig."

He began laughing the way he had done on the previous two occasions. But it was louder and hoarser than before. And there were the old tears running down his cheeks. Clare began to howl and that subdued him a bit, but he was still sniggering when he spoke to me.

"Remember, not a word to Maura or you'll be a dead man."

"Better dead than live in such dishonour."

"You fuck my wife and you talk of dishonour. Are you honouring me by fucking my wife?"

"Please don't use that word. It's obscene."

"You find another word for it. You are an educated man—a professor. You find me another word."

"Well, if you want another term, what we have between us is. . . "

I couldn't think of anything, when the phrase "religious liaison" came to mind. "What we have between us is religious liaison," I pronounced gravely. I think the phrase unconsciously summed up the sanctity of the relationship that existed between Maura and me, something I could hardly expect him to understand.

"Religious what?" he queried, with a stupefied look on his face. "Would you say that again? Never heard of it before. Fuck and screw are what we call it in this country.'

"I don't want to talk to you. You are the filthiest, dirtiest, meanest scoundrel I have ever known in my life."

"Is that true?"

"Yes, and I am sorry I ever came to this house."

"If you hadn't, where would you have got your fuck?"

"Stop it," I screamed.

Clare, who had quietened down, began to cry again. I took her from Ralph's arms and kissed her and pacified her. I gave her back to Ralph and asked him to tell Maura that I was going away for ever and would not be back again. This seemed to frighten him, for he changed his tone quickly.

"Look, old boy, I am not against your fucking my wife. If you didn't fuck her someone else would. I am philosophic about such things. All I want you to do is pay for the fuck. Why should I support her and pay the rent while you have a free ride?"

"Stop using your filthy language," I shouted. And then I added softly, but foolishly, "I buy her the groceries."

'What about buying me some?" he leapt at the opportunity. "I like abalone, succotash, zucchini and calamari."

"You are a swine and there's no denying it."

"All right, professor. I'm a swine. But let's settle this. You marry Maura. She is a fine woman and will make you a good wife: loyal, kind, noble, generous—you name it. And Clare is a lovely kid. You like her—I've seen you give her suck. You can have them both, they are yours from today. And I'll make you a king-size bed for a wedding gift. What do you say to that?"

"Who are you to give them to me? If I think it's appropriate, and Maura wishes it, we'll get married. We don't need your permission and you keep out."

"Professor, you forget that she's still my wife. What will your principal say when he comes to know what you are doing with my wife?"

"Are you trying to blackmail me?"

"Me? No, no. I only want you to understand my feelings. I want you to see how much I have suffered peeping through that hole and seeing her ride you. I want you to know how my heart bleeds to hear my own daughter call you Papa." And he began laughing again.

I took Clare in my arms, pressed her to my chest, kissed her several times, and with a heavy heart and tears running down my cheeks I handed her back to Ralph. I then ran out. I could hear Ralph calling after me, "Professor . . . Professor, don't mind what's happened. We are friends. Don't tell her anything—just marry her. Everything will be OK."

10

The phone rang incessantly all afternoon and evening, but I did not pick it up. The moment of decision had been forced upon me by the morning's events and I could delay it no longer. I wish Enright were here for me to consult him, though it would be impossible to get any sense out of him. He would merely put his feet on the desk and say, "Think, Tristan, think." I can think without his asking me. I may not be the wisest man in the world, but I am no fool either. Of that at least I am sure. Ralph had shattered the balance of my life with the unsavoury word "fuck." An innocent and pure love had been vulgarized, a spiritual experience had been made to sound something sinful and demeaning.

What was I to do now? Ralph was quite capable of going to the Principal with his story, and how would that affect my future. I wasn't really afraid of the Principal. I could ask him to keep his hands off a matter concerning my academic freedom, and I could count on full support from the Faculty Association which had just been unionized and was searching for a foolproof test case for a showdown with the administration. I could also depend on considerable student support because of the recent hike in their tuition fees. But what I dreaded was Peabody's cough and his holy stare. I could picture him standing in front of his desk—grave, stern, inexorable, his head moving in negation and the tassel of his mortarboard flipping from one ear to the other.

Much as I detested Ralph, I did not fail to acknowledge the

skill with which he had laid his trap to ensnare me and the absolute mastery with which he had played his hand. First, there was the hole over the bed, covered with soiled sheets so that no one should go near it. Then there was the saxophone into which he periodically blew (no doubt to let off steam) when the nightly drama became unbearable. There was the patient wait for the day Maura would be away so he could waylay me. He kept Clare on hand to lure me should I decide to flee on seeing him. Then, once having caught me, he states his premises in a phrase which is both a plea and an accusation: "Please stop fucking my wife." As I recover from the shock and provide him with a better alternative with which to sum up my relationship with his wife, he suggests that I marry her. Either to make the offer attractive or else to bribe me, he proposes to give me a king-size bed. Seeing that I am incorruptible, he uses a threat—what would my Principal think of my relationship with his wife? When he finds that I am rooted in righteousness and fear God and no one else, he quickly changes his tactics and pleads on compassionate grounds—the suffering he had to undergo peeping through the hole.

I felt that he deserved his suffering and ought to suffer more. My only regret was that I had inadvertently got entangled with a worthless character because of my love for Maura. And to rid myself of him I might have to give up Maura and Clare. To my eternal shame I toyed with this idea, but let it be said to my credit that I did so for not more than a minute. Sure I could walk out on Maura and Clare, but where would I go? Whose laundry would I wash? Whose house would I clean? For whom would I buy groceries? And what would I do with the breast shield in my pocket? I'd be completely lost without Maura and Clare. I might temporarily survive without Maura, but I couldn't live without Clare. There is something so sublime, so mystical, so other-worldly about her that I cannot give shape to it in words, but I can feel her divine presence.

And, then, could there be a greater display of cowardice than that I should desert Maura and Clare, both of whom need me, so that I could escape Ralph. Far from leaving them to this heartless pervert, it was my heaven-bound duty to protect them. "What would Solomon have done in my place?" I asked myself, and did not wait for an answer. I'd get Maura to move her bed to another part of the room, and I'd propose marriage to her.

11

Maura asked me where I had been all yesterday. I asked her if Clare had missed me.

"Not that I know of," she replied. "I've been trying to get hold of you. We are going to have our annual meeting of the Woman's Lib next week, and we want your help to rent the College Hall. It's going to be a big affair and we want a place that will hold 5,000 people."

I told Maura that I had business on hand more important than the meeting of the Women's Lib. She looked at me as if she could scarcely believe it, but said nothing. It was perhaps the urgency in my voice and the way my lower lip quivered, that discouraged her from challenging me.

"We've known each other for a long time, Maura."

"About six weeks."

"Not as long as some people have known each other. Do you trust me?"

"You're all I have, Tristan."

"That's good. You can do something for me without asking for an explanation."

"I'll try."

"No it should be a promise. You'll do what I ask you without questioning me. For once only."

"What is it?"

"Move your bed to another part of the room."

"Why?"

For a moment I thought I should tell Maura that Ralph had

been spying on us. But I was afraid she might blaze up, and that Ralph was mean enough to carry out his threat.

"You promised not to ask."

"Did I?"

"Yes, come let's move the bed."

We pulled the bed to the opposite side of the room. "We'll have more privacy here," I breathed, raising my eyes to the ceiling.

"Tristan, you are getting crazier and crazier every day. Who'd want to invade our privacy?"

"There are more things in heaven and earth than are dreamt of in your philosophy." And slapping my hand on the bed, I added, "Come, sit here."

Maura came and sat beside me. I asked her to take off her shoes and pull her feet up on the bed. I pressed her feet, and asked:

"Do you believe in marriage?"

"I did once. Why else would I have married that shit upstairs?"

"Will you marry me?"

"Are you proposing"

"Yes."

"What's the matter with you?'

"Nothing's the matter with me. I love you and Clare and I want to save you. . ."

"Save me? Save me from what?"

"I want to give you a home and security."

"On your salary? And with the alimony you are paying your wife?"

I had forgotten about that—I had quite forgotten I was a married man with a child.

"I'll divorce Elsa. Then we'll get married."

"No, we won't."

"Why not?"

"Elsa, too, is my sister. Have you asked her if she wants a divorce? You'll divorce her and marry me! What next? You'll divorce me and marry someone else. What are we women? Objects you men can marry and divorce at will?

I reminded her that it was Elsa who had left me—and that too when I was sick and in hospital; that she had taken my boy away and had not so much as sent me a get-well card, though I had been paying her $400 a month. For all I knew she might be dead and I might not even need a divorce.

But I failed to convince Maura. She was now full throttle on the subject of marriage and I could see she had heard and spoken a lot about it. Marriage is odious, marriage is exploitation, marriage is slavery, marriage is rape, marriage is everything but what it should be.

"For too long you people have exercised a brutal power over us in the name of marriage. You propose marriage to us as if it were your birthright. Why is it frowned upon for girls to propose marriage? Why can't I propose marriage to you?"

"What's stopping you?"

"My experience with that bum upstairs."

"What did he do to make you so bitter?"

"I don't want to talk about him."

"Was he good in bed?"

She thought for a while, and said: "Yes, that he was. But everything with him was a big joke—marriage, love, sex, everything. Something to laugh at! If he saw his mother dying, he'd laugh. When he made love to me . . . I shouldn't be telling you this."

"What harm if you did?"

"I guess none. He'd make me sing."

"What song?"

"He made it up himself. said it helped him with the erection if I sang while he made love."

"But what song?"

"You really want to hear it? I won't sing it, though. The words go something like this:

Ralph is the best fucker in town.
He goes longer, stronger every time
While others go down.
Ralph is the best fucker in town . . .

"And you sang that song?" I said, simmering with jealousy.

"I had to. He would stop in the middle of our love-making and say he couldn't go on unless I sang. He's a big bully. You don't know, Tristan, what I have gone through with that man. I didn't pick Women's Lib from out of a hat. I saw that women must unite if they are to protect themselves."

"I'd like to know one thing about Ralph. Is he a Peeping-Tom?"

"I don't care whether he is or not. But he is terribly curious. Before we were married we'd often have a shower together. He'd run out after a minute and sit on his haunches outside the bathroom door and peep through the keyhole. 'What's there to see in me?' I'd ask. 'Why not come in and enjoy your shower?' "

"That tells a lot about him," I remarked.

"Has he been saying anything to you?"

"No, though I'm sure he'd like us to get married."

"He sure would. He'd prefer anything to supporting his wife and kid."

"Look, Maura. Why not free yourself from him. I want a family, children, a brother for Clare, and we can't have those things as long as you remain his wife. If you are against marriage, you should be in favour of divorce."

"I'm in favour of divorce. But I first want him to recognize that Clare's his child."

"He may not be her father!"

"What!" she yelled. "Who then is her father? Your worthy self?"

"Who was Jesus's father?"

"Tristan, you better get your head examined—you better get to Enright, right away."

"I knew you'd say that. It is so easy to call other people mad. But would name-calling change anything? You may laugh at me, Maura, but there is something about Clare which makes me feel that she may be . . ."

"Go on."

"I said, 'may be.' "

"OK , 'may be.' Now say it."

"She *may be* the Messiah promised in the Old Testament," I blurted out, laying the stress on the "may be" as much as I could. And I shut my eyes so as not to see the ridicule such a proposition might invite. When I opened my eyes Maura was staring at me, and she continued to stare. Then she pointed her finger at Clare sitting on the potty and said, "That constipated brat?"

"The scriptures don't say a Messiah can't be constipated. Most holy men in India—sadhus, yogis, mahatmas—are not only constipated but suffer from chronic piles."

"What makes you so sure she is a Messiah?"

"Maura, don't twist my words. I only said, 'she may be.' I think if God were to send somebody to save the world, it is more likely he'd send his daughter this time."

"A daughter might certainly do more good, seeing the mess you men have made of the world."

"What mess are you talking about?"

"Look around—don't ask me. Look at the state of the world! Look at the inflation—look at the price of ground beef!"

"You women gave birth to men. Why blame us?"

"That's a nice way to pass the buck."

"I'm not passing the buck. Whatever happens to the world, the responsibility rests equally on both men and women. If you housewives will only stop buying beef, the price will come down."

"It's silly to argue with you, Tristan."

"Let's stop arguing and get on with our work. Clare is your child and I love her dearly. And for her sake I beg you to get a divorce."

"All right, I'll get a divorce."

"And marry me?"

"No, Tristan. I don't believe in marriage any more, and I want my freedom. But if you like, we can live together"

"That's OK with me. When do I move in?"

"You don't move in. We wait till you get back to your job and can afford to rent a house."

"That shouldn't take too long. Say, do we have children?"

"Why not? Vanessa has two boys and she's been single all her life. Roxanne and Mathilda have a daughter each."

"Who are Roxanne and Mathilda?'

"My sisters. You'll meet them at the Annual. The meeting is open to all men and women sympathetic to our cause. We want it to be a big success, and I want you to help us. We are expecting delegates from all over—from Montana and North Dakota and from other places."

"How do I help?"

"Stand beside me, Tristan. Let the world see that we women are not alone in this struggle—that every intelligent and right-minded man is with us. We are not a bunch of kooks who go about waving flags and shouting everything down. We are an organized group fighting male exploitation for a just society."

"I'll stand by you."

"You also take complete charge of publicity and arrangements." And she told me that renting the hall, putting the ads in the paper, preparing handbills and posters, inviting the press, and arranging the seating for 5,000 people would be my sole responsibility. I was to take orders from no one but her.

12

Today is the big day. I have worked my ass off to make it a success. I have been so busy that I have breast-fed Clare only twice in the past week. The laundry remains unwashed, and the pots and pans are stacked high in the kitchen sink. We have been living on MacDonald's hamburgers, for Maura hasn't had the time to cook. As Convener and Master of Ceremonies, she's on the phone or on her feet eighteen hours a day. She has hardly said a loving word to me except "do this" or "do that."

Maura wants the Goddess Durga to be adopted as the symbol of the Erigon chapter of the Women's Lib. But for all my efforts, I have failed to locate a picture of the Goddess. I have suggested to Maura that as a makeshift arrangement we use one of her photographs and I'll get an artist friend of mine, a guy called Martell, to draw ten arms on it. Maura likes my suggestion but fears that some of her sisters, who are already jealous of her, might criticize her for self-aggrandizement.

I have spent not only all my time, but a pretty penny on the Annual Meeting. The rent for the hall alone came to $200, which I paid. (Maura has assured me that I will be reimbursed from what they collect as entrance fees. It is fifty cents a head.) I also put two announcements of the Annual in *The Hemisphere* and wrote personal letters to the newspaper editors across Canada to make a careful note of the date and not to forget to send their representatives. I spent a tidy sum buying paper and coloured pencils for the posters and drove all over the city distributing handbills and occasionally, when the police were not around, announced over the loudspeaker the day, place and time of the meeting.

We came to the hall at six—an hour before the meeting was to start. We wanted to be in time to receive the early comers and have them seated in an orderly fashion. Besides, there might be some last minute arrangements, though I had personally attended to every aspect of the meeting—from microphones to sanitary towels in the bathrooms. I insisted on taking Clare with me for I had done my part of the work, and all that remained for me was to find an empty seat, relax and enjoy the lectures with Clare in my lap.

Soon after we arrived, the old red van pulled up and about a dozen women jumped out. They all wore frayed blue jeans, but had on shirts of different colours. None of them wore makeup, and some of them were barefoot. I liked the way they stood with their hands on their hips, jabbing each other in the ribs with their elbows as they spoke and laughed. Maura seemed a little inhibited before them; so did a woman in her early forties who came riding a bike. Dressed in a black shirt, she had a sweet, sad face and was less boisterous than the others. Her name was Frances, and she was the secretary of WOOW (World Organization of Older Women).

Maura introduced me to her friends: to Vanessa, self-styled Field Commander of SKAM (Society for Killing All Men); Roxanne, Secretary General of WITCH (Women's Invincible Terrorist Campaign from Hell); Matilda, President of FAW (Facts About Women); and Barbara, Vice-president of SOL (Sisters of Lesbos). She also introduced me to a meek little girl called Sandy, who occasionally baby-sat for her and had genuine affection for Clare. Sandy sat beside me in the meeting and took care of Clare when I was invited to the dais.

Ten minutes after seven, Maura called the meeting to order, requesting the audience to move up to the first two rows which had been reserved for the press. Not a single representative of the press had come, and the total audience numbered no more than sixty. Of these, seven were middle-aged men and the rest mostly women in their late twenties and thirties.

Vanessa, who sat on the dais with the other leaders, accused me of poor organization and publicity. Maura immediately rose to my defence, pointing out that I had spent over $200 from my pocket and, since the collection from the gate was under $30 (some had got in free), I stood to lose all the money I had invested. She blamed the poor turnout on male conspiracy against their Movement and said I was blameless. This silenced Vanessa, and there were a few hand claps for me and Frances called out "Thanks, Tristan." It pained me, however, to learn I wouldn't get my money back, but Maura's vindication of me was fair recompense.

The meeting opened with Maura reminding the audience that their strength lay not in their numbers but in their convictions—that each day the Movement was growing and affecting the lives of women in countries as distant as Peru and Papua New Guinea. But as Master of Ceremonies, it wasn't for her to give a lecture, but call on the distinguished speakers to enlighten an equally distinguished audience. But before she did so, she would request the audience to stand up and sing a recent song by a renowned feminist.

We all stood up and sang. It was murderous, and few of us knew the words, but it had a stanza in it which electrified the audience and was repeated several times with tremendous gusto:

Be a good sister,
Join in the fight.
Say "drop dead" to your mister,
He is the cause of your plight.

After the song Maura said that the Executive of the Women's Lib had selected the Goddess Durga, through the good offices of Tristan, as their symbol. She described what Durga looks like and how she slays men and demons. However, as she could not find a picture of the Goddess, the approval of the symbol would not be put to vote until the next meeting.

The first person to address us was Barbara of the Daughters of Lesbos. She had beautiful, long legs. She twice strode from one end of the dais to the other in a contemplative manner, paused before the mike and, tossing up her head, said, "Sisters and brothers, I'm proud to say I'm menstruating today!" She then kicked at the mike, came and stood at the edge of the dais and spoke to us for forty minutes.

Her subject was sexual emancipation. Women could not be wholly emancipated until they accepted their bodily functions with dignity and wiped away the false notions impregnated in their minds by a male society. "I'm not proud to menstruate," she added a little later, "but if I am to menstruate, I'm not ashamed of it. Menstruation may be bothersome, but it is not filthy as some male habits are: their whoring and drinking, the way they shake their penises dry after urinating."

She next turned to Freud. She called him the most "pompous of asses" for thinking that women had penis envy. "To envy a man his penis is like envying a camel it's hump," she said and paused for applause. She challenged Freud to come forward and prove his theory that a girl at puberty transfers the centre of orgasm from the clitoris to the vagina. "There is no such fuckin' thing as vaginal orgasm," she thundered, while Maura nodded approvingly. And she cited her own findings as proof that the most intense orgasms are achieved by masturbatory methods.

That Barbara was a practised orator one could see from the way she linked masturbation with the advantages of being a Lesbian. "Lesbianism involves physical love between women. Who among you would deny that love between equals is more pleasurable than gratifying the sexual wants of an oppressor?"

"None, none," said several from the audience.

"Because of her ability to obtain love and sex from her own kind, the Lesbian does not have to depend on men. She is no longer required to do menial chores for them like wash their underpants. She does not have to cater to their oversized egos nor condone their 'going, going, gone' sexual encounters. Above all, she is freed from the fear of unwanted pregnancy, the pains of childbirth, and the sheer drudgery of child rearing."

"Child rearing is no drudgery," I called out, standing up with Clare in my arms. "Happy is the woman who hath her quiver full of them."

"Don't interrupt the speaker," cried Matilda.

"I will," I retorted. "Let no one sin against the child."

"What do you know about child rearing?" Barbara railed at me. "You're never gone through labour pains—you've never given suck to a baby."

"How can you be so sure?" I asked.

Maura was quick to react. She asked me to shut up and sit down. I protested against the lie and reminded her how hard I had worked for the success of the meeting and that I had a right to be heard.

"Shut up, Tristan," she yelled at me. "One more word and out you go."

I sat down. I decided not to pay any more attention to the speakers. What sort of justice was one to expect from these women if they ever got into power? They who talk about their rights and deny me mine!

The second speaker was Vanessa. She would have looked prettier if she hadn't been so angry. I didn't take note of her until she was half-way through her tirade. I would have ignored her completely if it had not been for her repeated use of that obnoxious word "fuck."

"We women have been fucked into seeing how fucking evil man is. And we now realize that we have as much fucking ability as the best of them. Fuck is the word: and fuck, fuck, fuck makes the world go round. Parents fuck you up, schools fuck you up, doctors fuck you up, jobs fuck you up . . ."

Vanessa's prophylactic for all this fucking is to eliminate man altogether and assume full mastery of the state. The

SKAM members, she foresees, will become soldiers of the "unwork force, the fucked-up force." They will bring the government to a standstill by seeing that not a penny goes into its coffers. SKAM bus drivers won't charge fares, SKAM police officers won't issue speeding tickets, SKAM senators won't pass legislation. SKAM will kill all men who do not subscribe to the aims of the SKAM politburo.

Vanessa's speech scared the hell out of the few men who were present. Maura, who is very perceptive, saw the fear on their faces and assured them that Women's Lib wishes to live in peace with them and that they would not be exterminated except as a last resort. As for me, I felt sorry for Vanessa. She must have come across a beast like Ralph, or why else would she want to exterminate all men? Poor girl, if only she had had the good fortune to meet me before I had known Maura, she'd be all flowers today. As I couldn't give her my love, I thought I'd get her to see my doctor in Kamsack. She'd surely appreciate that.

The third speaker was Frances from the World Organization of Older Women. She spoke in personal terms and not for more than five minutes. She did not curse men and that put her at a disadvantage. Besides, she couldn't seem to relate to the audience. "I am forty-four, " she said. "I am twice the age of most of you, but that doesn't mean I have no feelings. Yesterday my daughter told me, 'Mum, you're not old.' But I am. I am old and bitter and frustrated. I see half my adult life stretch before me, empty of love, of friendship, even of hope. To the men I am no longer desirable—and I don't blame them. But you, my sisters, must you leave me behind because I am old and tired and can no longer keep step with you? I have tried, I have tried hard . . ." She didn't finish what she wanted to say, but pulled out a Kleenex from her purse and began to wipe her eyes. I clapped my hands to encourage her to continue at which she started sobbing.

The next speaker, Matilda of FAW, brought forth a number of charges against men and institutions. She followed up by presenting a series of demands, and I wasn't sure whether we were supposed to grant them, for who else would! Matilda had a lot of horrifying statistics on female exploitation which would make so much jelly of Ripley's *Believe It or Not.* I began to take down notes when Sandy said that the information was at least a hundred years old.

The last speaker of the evening was the WITCH, Roxanne. I was dozing off into a comfortable slumber when I heard her call out, "Let the strongest man among you come forward."

"I opened my eyes and looked at her. I didn't know what the invitation was for. I turned to the men and saw they were looking sheepishly at one another.

"Will the strongest and bravest of you come up on the dais?" Roxanne said again.

I was wondering if I should volunteer myself when Roxanne called out my name. I stood up and caught Maura's gaze. With a quick shake of her head she asked me to desist. But the audience was now all excited and people were saying, "Well done . . . brave lad. Up, go up . . ." I handed Clare to Sandy and climbed up on the dais amidst cheers.

I stood facing Roxanne. She was huge, broad-chested, and about thirty.

"Come, attack me. Come, come," she said. And keeping her eyes fixed on me, she began sliding around me on her big feet.

I moved towards her gingerly with my arms stretched in front of me, not so much to attack her as to keep my distance from her.

"Come, come, attack me," she kept saying as I followed her cautiously. Seeing that I wasn't being aggressive enough, she undid the buttons of her shirt and showed me her breasts.

"Come, come, take my boobs," she cajoled.

All this merely confused me, and I asked her what I was supposed to do.

"Think yourself a rapist. Rape me—fuck me."

I turned my back to the audience to undo my zipper.

"No, no, not that," she said grimacing.

"How am I to rape you, then?" I asked.

"Come. Fuck me, rape me, take my boobs" she repeated, dancing around me and sliding away every time I made an effort to get close to her.

The audience laughed and cheered and shouted. "Move on, Tristan. Get to her . . . she's a prize. Come on . . . be a man. Take her in your arms—crush her."

I began moving faster, chasing her all over the dais with my arms stretched forward. I managed to throw a sidelong glance at Maura, who shook her head discreetly to signify "no." But the euphoria of the audience had quite infected me, and the pleas of "fuck me. . . rape me" were clanging like church bells in my ears. I made a sudden dash for her breasts—

I shot through the air. I found myself on the floor, breathless. Maura tried to get me back on my feet, but I begged her to leave me alone. I thought I had broken my spinal column. Clare began to howl, and as a last request I asked that she be brought and placed near me. It quietened her. Someone suggested that I be covered with a sheet so that I did not catch a chill lying on the floor. I protested.

Roxanne lectured on the scientific and psychological principles behind karate, urging all females between ten and seventy to learn it for self-defence. "I've demonstrated how every one of you can protect yourself against a dangerous rapist like him," she said, pointing at me. And she asked the audience to sing after her the WITCH's famous incantation:

Double, bubble, war and rubble,
If you mess with women, you'll be in trouble.

The meeting concluded with Maura asking for a vote of thanks. She thanked everybody for making the Annual a success. She mentioned me by name and expressed appreciation for the hard work I had put in. The audience rose to its feet to give me a standing ovation, and I was deeply touched by their warmth and gratitude and waved to them from where I lay.

Sandy saw us home. She drove my car while I lay on the back seat holding Clare. She said Roxanne hadn't floored me according to the rules of the game—she had merely clobbered me. She had kicked me, boxed my ears, pulled my nose, slapped me on both cheeks, and thrown me over her shoulder on to the floor. That wasn't karate.

13

"Don't be so sad, Tristan," said Maura, placing an order for Southern fried chicken. I ordered tomato soup and a bottle of white wine. My throat was too dry for me to swallow anything else.

"Cheer up. It's your birthday," she coaxed.

"July the 29th! Of all the days in the year, why should it have happened today?"

"Don't worry, I'll be pregnant soon."

"It still can't bring back the baby we've lost," I said, trying to hold back my tears.

"I don't think I was pregnant after all. The menses were delayed."

"By two full weeks! No, my love, let's not deceive ourselves. the Lord hath given and the Lord hath taken away. Blessed be the name of the Lord."

"But how can you be so sure that I was pregnant?"

I told her that I had been quietly making a study of pregnancy and childbirth, and that every morning before coming to her place I went to the college library to read up on the subject. The symptoms she had shown in the past two weeks were clearly those of early pregnancy. She was passing urine frequently; I spent two nights with her especially to observe this phenomenon. She had become lethargic; she was not doing her share of the household work and had slackened up on cooking. Her breasts had become swollen and tender; I had felt them myself and couldn't doubt my own hands. She must be having pains in the back for she rode me mostly at a trot. She suffered from nausea; she threw up the lamb curry I had cooked for her the other day. And, lastly, she had been very moody and off-handish towards me.

"I'll admit to the moodiness," she said. "I am fond of you, Tristan, but there are times I feel smothered. You are with me every day from morning till night. There are times when I want to be by myself. It is to preserve my independence that I don't get married. But what independence do I have?"

I ignored her last remark. She had lately been talking about independence as if she were Quebec herself.

"I even experienced the syptoms some men do when their wives are pregnant," I continued.

"What symptoms?"

"Morning sickness."

The food arrived. We were halfway through our meal when Martell, the moon painter, came rushing up to our table. He was about fifty, stocky, with a pink face and platinum blonde eyebrows. He always spoke in whispers as if he were confiding a secret. His small eyes were like those of a zealot and gave urgency to whatever he said.

"Have you been out, Tristan?" he asked in a hushed voice.

"Yes. Why?"

"It's a full moon," he whispered conspiratorially in my ear.

"Here, meet Maura," I said. "Maura, this is my friend Martell."

Maura smiled a big "hello," but Martell was too engrossed to take notice of her. She flushed red at the insult.

"Would you give me a ride to the Flying Club?" he asked.

You're not flying tonight—are you?"

"Shh. I want to give the moon a closer look." And he looked around furtively to make sure nobody had heard him. "I'll be back in fifteen minutes," he said, and disappeared before I could say anything.

Maura rebuked me for having a boor like Martell for a friend and then wanted to know everything about him. I told her that he is a painter of moons, that he has painted moons since he was a kid, that he has painted nothing else but moons. He has painted moons of every colour, but his most precious piece is a black moon in a white sky. It is thought to be priceless—in fact no one has ever made an offer to buy it. As for the other moons, he would sell one or two a year. Then in 1969 came the boom—the Americans landed a man on the moon. The liberals of Erigon made a beeline to Martell's studio and bought off all his moons except the red ones. Soon after, the Russians put a rocket on the moon. All the Marxist-Leninists, who had earlier scoffed at his moons, now tumbled over one another to buy his red ones. During the next four years, as the two super-powers fought for the moon with men and rockets, Martell painted like a demon and made a fast buck. But his luck was too good to last; the Americans and the Russians turned to battle for more distant planets and Martell's sales dwindled. Today he hardly sells a painting; he spends his time pub-crawling. That is if he is not in hospital.

"Was he too with you in Kamsack?"

"Maura, he'd never forgive you if he heard that. It's *we* who were with him; he was almost always there. He knew the doctors and the nurses and made us feel at home. Occasionally, when one of us would cry and want to get out, he'd cheer us up with, "Hell—what's there outside?"

When Martell returned, I asked him if he couldn't hitch a ride with someone else—today being a special occasion for us. Maura intervened saying that since we had finished our meals we might as well drop Martell off at the Flying Club and then go for a drive in the moonlight. So we got into my car, Martell insisting on sitting alone in the back seat. All along the way he did not utter a single word but kept staring at the moon. When we got to the Club he asked me if I'd care to go up with him. I said, "No." He then asked if my missus would like to go up. I told him that she wasn't legally my missus and that she wouldn't want to go up.

"Let me speak for myself," Maura said to me sharply. And

then coyly to Martell, "I'd love to go up—I've never been in an airplane before."

"You wouldn't like it, Maura," I said quickly to keep Martell away from her. "You feel crammed in. And even when you're going up, you can't help feeling you're going down."

I failed to dissuade Maura. She wanted to look at the earth from the sky, and I couldn't convince her that it was safer to look at the sky from the earth. I finally gave in and asked Martell how long he would be up.

He looked steadily at the moon for a minute, did some fast calculations on his fingers, and said it would be a couple of hours. As it was already nine, I suggested to Maura that I go home and relieve the baby-sitter Sandy while she could get back in a taxi after the trip. She was delighted and began hopping on her toes the way little girls do.

It was close to one and no sign of Maura. I kept the radio on for the worst news, though most of the stations had gone off the air for the remainder of the night. The plane had crashed—of that there was no doubt. Whether Maura was dead or crippled still remained to be determined. As I couldn't bear the idea of Maura dead, I prayed that she be crippled for life. My voice choked with grief, I spoke each word aloud for God to hear. Ralph poked his head at me from up the stairs and said that he wanted to sleep and I should ease up on God. I ignored him and continued with my prayers.

I was crossing myself "In the name of the Father" when Maura stole on me quietly and asked me what I was doing. I turned around and saw her standing on her own two feet! "The Lord be praised!" I cried.

"What's the matter?" she asked me.

"I couldn't bear the idea of your being dead. So I was praying that you be crippled for life."

"Why should I be crippled for life?"

"Life in any form is better than death. Clare needs you and I need you."

"I don't understand."

I told her that when it was eleven and she hadn't returned, I began to fear the worst. And my worst fears were realized in the next two hours—the plane had crashed. I had gone down on my knees and prayed to the Almighty to keep her safe. "O Heavenly Father, put her in a wheelchair and give her to me. I'll push her around until I die." These were my very words—she could ask Ralph. He heard me and asked me to shut up.

"But couldn't you pray that nothing should happen to me?"

"I never thought of that. When one is in love, one always expects the worst."

"You fool!" she laughed. "I should have phoned you and said I'm OK."

"From the sky?"

"No, we never did go up. The Club wouldn't let him lease a plane."

"Where did you go?"

"We went back to Sandra's for coffee"

"You went back to Sandra's! You sat for four hours over a cup of coffee?" I asked, unable to believe my ears.

"No, we had several cups. Why do you question me like that?"

"On my birthday you went to Sandra's with another man! You spent the last hours of my birthday with another man!"

"We were together the whole day, weren't we?"

"My one birthday—my only birthday in the year," I lamented. "And you spent it with a stranger!"

"Isn't he your friend?"

"Here I was killing myself pushing your wheelchair while you . . ."

"Stop pushing the wheelchair, will you?" she lashed at me.

"Don't shout," I shouted back. "You go out with a looney on my birthday and then shout at me."

"I'll go with whoever I want."

"No, you won't. Not when you are mine."

"I am not yours. I am my own boss—you get that straight."

"You are not your own boss. The Lord hath said, 'Thy desire shall be thy husband, and he shall rule over thee'."

I shouldn't have repeated what the Lord said, but I had been praying for a long time and in the process had gone holy. Maura exploded:

"You are not my husband."

"'Wives, submit yourselves unto your husbands, as unto the Lord. For the husband is the head of the wife . . .' What say you to that?"

"Just this: you get out of my house."

"Now?"

"Right now. Get out, get out . . ." she yelled at the top of her voice.

There was the sound of footsteps, and we waited in silence. We saw Ralph coming down the stairs slowly, holding a bottle of beer. He was stark naked, and his penis stuck out like a small tulip bulb below his belly.

"What's all this hullabaloo about?" he asked.

"Go and put on your pyjamas," I said in a commanding voice to win Maura's approval. "You are in the presence of a lady."

"Lady, my foot! She's my fuckin' wife."

"Get the hell out of here," screamed Maura, striking him with one hand and shoving him up the stairs with the other.

"I'm going, I'm going," entreated Ralph, as he tried to save his beer from spilling. "Aye, girl, mind the precious liquid."

"Hold on, Maura. I'll see that he goes up," I said, coming between her and Ralph.

I thought that by taking her side I'd be able to restore myself to her good graces. But I was wrong. She began to shove me up the stairs as well, hurling foul abuse at the same time. From halfway up the stairs Ralph watched us with amusement.

Clare began to cry and I instinctively unbuttoned my shirt. Maura looked at me with amazement, as if I were a blessed apparition from heaven, and then began shouting again:

"Out, get out, Tristan. Get out, get out . . ."

Ralph came down and took me by the wrist. He began to lead me up the stairs. I wouldn't have gone with him for all the world had Maura not pushed me from behind with a broom.

14

Ralph sat on the edge of the bed with his feet dangling. I squatted opposite him on the floor.

"Well, Professor, what can I do for you?" he asked.

I told him that I would like him to get into his pyjamas. He said he didn't have any. I said he could slip on his underpants. He said he had washed them and they were drying in the bathroom. And as for getting into his trousers, he wouldn't do it for the Pope himself.

"In that case I must leave you," I said.

"Wait," he said, standing up. "Have a beer."

I accepted the beer on the condition that he would hide his nakedness. He took a shirt and wrapped it round his waist, insisting that he did so only because he respected me as a professor and his future husband-in-law. I said I doubted if Maura would be mine again, and I told him all about the moon painter and how he had sneaked into my life and wrecked it.

"That's bad, Tristan. But, don't worry. You're the best donkey she ever rode, and though she may whip your ass, she knows your worth."

"I hope you're right, though I'm afraid she might ride Martell now," I moaned.

"I won't let her," he consoled me. "I'm her husband."

"How can you stop her?"

"I'll blow the saxophone. I'll blow and I'll blow till I burst, but I won't let her ride him."

"That's if you find out! How will you?"

"Brother, move a little to your right and look through the hole you are sitting on."

I obeyed. I saw Maura lying on her stomach with her legs wide apart. Her tiny buttocks stood out, and I fought back a tremendous urge to go and kiss her and make her into a flower girl again.

"I wonder when she moved the bed back," I said at last.

"She didn't. I had to drill a fresh hole. If you folks keep moving the bed it will make a colander of my floor."

"You swine!" I hissed. And I stood up to leave.

"Take it easy, brother. You won't get Maura by swining me. I am the only man who can get you Maura. From now on you'll have to treat me with respect. Right?"

"How?"

"You'll have to call me Mr Ralph."

"Mr Ralph," I said.

"Nobody has ever called me mister before. You are the first person to call me mister. My granny used to say, 'When others don't respect you, you lose all respect for yourself.' That's what happened to me—I lost self-respect. But now I've got it back, thanks to you, Tristan."

"How do I get Maura back, Mr Ralph?"

"Have another beer, first," he said going to the fridge. He opened the bottle with the heel of a boot and gave it to me. He continued:

"Maura is like a musical instrument. She is, you might say, like the saxophone. You get the most beautiful music out of her if you know how to play her stops."

He gave a long discourse on Maura's character, observing what a kind and gentle person she was and what a "super" wife she'd make me—things I already knew. But the one thing he said which I didn't know was that Maura always wanted to be on the top—whatever the thing might be. He told me how, when they were separating, Maura wanted the top floor of the house. He had great trouble convincing her that the ground floor had more space and would be better for the kid, who might fall down the stairs if she took the top floor. "Frankly, I couldn't care less for the kid," he confessed. "I wanted the top floor to keep Maura under surveillance."

I reminded him that he had not yet answered my question: how was he going to help me with Maura? He said that needed some thinking, but I could begin right away by doing nothing. By that he meant I should give her time to cool off—leave her alone for a while. Then, on a day Martell is visiting her, I should just walk in boldly and say "hello" to everybody and behave as if I were engaged to her and soon to get married. This would put her in a real bind and at the same time tell Martell to buzz off.

"But what if Martell doesn't come? He is too sold on the moon to take any interest in women. If he doesn't come I'll be ruined."

"Ah, Tristan, we must hope for the best. You could pray—couldn't you? You are chummy with God."

"I'll do that," I said, "but I don't want to be too long on the street waiting for Martell."

"No, no. You stay at home and wait for the telephone and I'll keep an eye out for Martell. As soon as he comes I'll phone you. You run down as fast as you can. I'll keep the front door open so you don't have to ring the bell, for the way she is now, she'll piss on you if she catches you alone. But in the presence of Martell she'll act a proper lady."

I told him that though his plan was excellent, I couldn't wait alone in my apartment. I needed to see Clare everyday. I couldn't live without Clare.

"Brother, if you are that far gone, why didn't you marry Maura and move in with her the day I gave you my blessings?" he asked.

I was explaining to him that Maura doesn't believe in marriage and won't let me move in with her, when he suddenly jumped and began to do the rumba on the bed. He said he had got a brilliant idea and I should give him my full attention. But first things first, we should each have another beer. And he fetched two more beers from the fridge.

"Tristan, are you ready?"

"Yes."

"Ready?"

"Yes."

"You move in with me. You can . . ."

"What! Move in with a man?"

"Don't interrupt, or I'll lose my idea. You can bring your own bed if you want, or you can have whichever side of my bed you like—left or right. Don't worry about that. You'll be close to Maura and Clare and you can watch out for Martell yourself. You can stay here till death do us part."

"It is very generous of you, Ralph, but . . ."

"Mr Ralph, with your pardon."

"Mr Ralph, Maura may not approve of my living with you."

"Hold on a bit—before I forget what I have to say. You can sleep on the floor and peep through the hole. I'll charge you room and board, but nothing for the hole. What do you say?"

I would have said no, but the thought of sleeping all night with my eyes glued to the hole was too much to resist. Besides, by staying with Ralph I would be near my dearest Clare. I wouldn't have to stay here very long, anyway. I'd soon be back at my job and I'd have my own house and my Maura and plenty of kids. I agreed.

"Now let's settle the rent," he said. "I'd keep you for nothing, but this inflation is hitting the poorest hardest. Look at the price of beer! Put up the price of hard liquor, I say, but not of soft drinks. On my income I can't afford solid foods and so I have to pee a lot. I have a rare disease called saliromania—that's what Dr Enright says."

"How much a month?" I asked in a businesslike fashion. I was prepared to pay up to $350.

"Say $250 a month! Or is that too much?"

"I'll pay you $300 a month," I said.

"You will!" he sang out getting up and kissing me on both cheeks. "Oh, brother Tristan, you are a swell guy—you are an

Indian prince. And the day is not far off when Maura will be your queen."

The deal settled, Ralph brought out six more bottles and uncapped them all at once. As I drank, I thought what a good-hearted and generous man Ralph was in spite of his crudity and how I had misjudged him. I was thinking of apologizing to him when he touched my heart with yet another kindness—he proposed we should seal the agreement between us with a "Happy birthday to you." I pointed out regretfully that my birthday was four hours gone now.

"Let's sing 'He's a jolly good fellow. . . ,' for that's what you really are, Tristan."

Ralph began singing, and after the first two refrains I joined in. Soon the room was resounding with our voices. As I sang full-throated I wished my Maura was there.

She was. She was standing in her underclothes at the door with the broom in her hand. One glance at her and my voice froze, but Ralph who hadn't seen her continued with the song. When it came to an end, he looked at me and I pointed to Maura with my eyes.

We three kept looking at each other for what must have been a long time. Then Maura broke the silence.

"Go home, Tristan." Her voice was so quiet and firm that I couldn't associate it with her.

"I can't," I replied. I looked at Ralph for support, but he sat with his eyes averted. "What about our deal?" I finally asked him.

"What deal?" he queried innocently. Before I could remind him, he brought his forefinger to his mouth to bid me to keep quiet.

I took the hint. I stood up and put out my hand for him to shake. "Good night Mr Ralph," I said.

"Mr Ralph!" Maura repeated the words and sniggered. "Did he tell you what else he learned from his granny?"

"Ralph is a gentleman," I declared, coming to the defence of my friend.

Maura did not contradict me. She merely took me by the ear and led me gently down the stairs. When we got to the front door, I asked her what groceries I should bring her in the morning. She looked at me with exasperation and was about to slam the door in my face when I called out "Darling." The word must have kindled loving memories in her, for instead of slamming the door in my face she hit me with the broom and wished me "Good night."

15

The phone made me jump. I gave a curse to whoever it might be for getting me out of bed this early in the morning.

"He's here," said the voice.

"Who's here? And who the hell are you?"

Ralph identified himself and said that the painter was there, or at least it seemed like him and he had come with a huge canvas and looked exactly as I had described him the previous night.

"Tell him to wait. I'll be down in no time," I said.

"You better hurry, Tristan, and establish your claim. I've done my job, and I don't want anything more to do with it. Don't tell Maura I phoned you. She was mad at me last night and I've washed my hands of her completely."

"Don't worry. Everything will be all right," I said to comfort him and then hung up.

I looked at my watch. It was two! I couldn't believe it and so I pulled back the curtains and saw the sun riding overhead. I had slept soundly in spite of my love for Maura. Within minutes I was ready, and I found the door of Maura's house unlatched to receive me.

"Hello, everybody," I said, exactly as Ralph had advised me. I didn't want to take any risks.

Maura and Martell were sitting at the kitchen table. Clare was in Martell's lap sucking his thumb.

Maura gave me a dirty look but no worse than the ones I have had before. Martell was in the middle of something he was expounding and did not even acknowlege my entry. But I quickly made my presence felt by snatching Clare from him and rebuking him:

"Where did you grow up? Don't you know that you don't put your dirty thumb in a child's mouth! You could give her an infection." And I pulled the bottom of my T-shirt out of my trousers and offered her my nipple. Clare wouldn't take it, but she smiled—the holy child.

Martell, it seems, was explaining the geology of the moon and how a painter must know the innards of the things he paints. He said he had spent as many years studying the moon's volume and density as he had spent studying its surface features: its mountains, craters, hills and valleys. He had not been able to show all these features owing to the lack of a sizeable canvas, but in his priceless black moon he had shown Mount Epsilon—which is higher than Mount Everest itself. "When you are painting an object that is moving around the earth at 2,287 miles per hour, you have to keep your wits about you," he confided. "And you have to take into consideration the moon's *sidereal* and *synodical* revolutions, not to mention its average *albedo*."

Maura was listening to him with rapt attention—the sort of attention she never gives to anything I have to say. This made me jealous and I decided to demolish Martell once and for all.

"Hey, Martell, when do you go to Kamsack again?"

"In about two hours," he replied, and began discoursing on the need to remap the lunar surface.

I was astonished at the bastard's cheekiness. I had thought that by reminding him he is a sick man I might be able to infuriate him, but here the fellow had dismissed me with a shrug. He had Maura's attention and he couldn't care less for me. Anyway, I decided that instead of insulting Martell I should get on with establishing my right over Maura.

"Maura, darling," I said, standing behind her chair and putting an arm around her neck, "should I book the VIP suite in Hotel Erigon for our honeymoon?"

"Get off my back," replied Maura, disengaging herself. Martell looked at me, but I could see that it hadn't registered in his dense mind that Maura and I were lovers. Maura asked him to continue with his discourse and he got on to his moon again.

"I think I shall have the diamond set in platinum. Or would you rather have a ring of rubies set in gold?"

"I'd rather you left, Tristan," she said, taking Clare from my arms.

"When I become Chairman of my Department, I'd have to give a lot of parties. It would be a busy life for you, my dear. But we'll keep a nanny to take care of our kids—I could easily afford one on my salary."

Maura did not reply, and Martell didn't take the least notice of what I said. I had never in my life come across a more crass and dim-witted man. Couldn't he see he wasn't wanted here? Couldn't he see that Maura was mine and there was no hope for him whatsoever?

Martell went on and on about the moon. I sat opposite him and kept saying "shit" every ten seconds. Maura asked me to "disappear" several times and muttered some nasty things under her breath which I positively refused to hear. I thought nothing short of Maura riding me at a gallop would register in Martell's mind that she was really mine, when he finally stood up to leave.

"I'll hang the painting before I go. Maura, get me a hammer and some nails," said Martell.

"What painting?" I asked.

"The black moon. I'm lending it to Maura for the time I'm away."

"We don't want the painting. It doesn't go with the decor of our living room."

"Don't pay any attention to him, Martell," said Maura, fetching a hammer and some nails.

Soon the painting was on the wall despite my protests. Martell and Maura stepped back to the opposite wall and began admiring it.

Martell kissed Maura on the forehead to wish her goodbye. Thank God he still had the hammer in his hand for, had it been in mine, I would have cracked his skull.

"I'll see you when I get back," Martell said to Maura.

"You won't," I rejoined. "She'll be pregnant by then."

"Fuck off, Tristan," Maura breathed in my ear and left the room. Ralph was right in assuming that in the presence of Martell she'd act a proper lady.

Martell put his hand on my shoulder and said, "You've got a fine girl there. Take care of her."

"I will," I swore. "This land is full of adulterers."

"That's for sure. But if ever anybody looks at Maura with an evil eye, you write to me and I'll come and lay him out."

"Write to you! Where are you going?"

"Didn't I tell you I'm off to Kamsack? Boy, I could see it coming. I phoned the doctor and he said I should get there right away."

"Are you serious?"

"Yes. That's why I came here—to say goodbye to Maura. And I thought I'd lend her the painting."

"I'm sorry," I mumbled.

"Sorry for what? I am sick of the lunatics in Erigon. Every few months I have to go to the hospital to regain my sanity. Kamsack is the place for us, Tristan. All my happy memories are associated with the place. Do you remember the first time you were there? You had a squirt-gun and you went bang-bang at the nurses: 'destroying the womb,' you said."

"I was crazy, then," I said, seeing him to the door with mixed feelings. On the one hand I felt sorry for the bastard; on the other, I felt he was responsible for the unhappiness he had brought between Maura and me. Instead of taking off for the moon, had he taken off for Kamsack a day earlier, things would have been different. But thank God it had all ended well.

When I got back, Maura was sitting on the floor of her living room holding her head. She seemed composed but was breathing heavily.

"Have you a headache, my love?"

"Go home, Tristan."

"Why?"

"Go home, please."

"What have I done? Why do you want me to go? Have you forgotten all our plans?"

"That's all over. Go home now. I am asking you for the tenth time to go home."

"No, sweet girl, for the third time only. I've been counting."

"Go away. You sicken me."

"I can't. You are my whole life—I love you."

"I'd be better off without your love," she said, raising her voice. And then quietly, and in a tone of icy coldness, "I don't love you. I've never loved you—believe me. I've never loved you. You forced yourself upon me. Now get out for God's sake."

"It will kill me."

"You are not to die here. If you did, I wouldn't know what to do with you. Out, out on the grass there. If you don't get out this minute, I'll call the police. Get out, get out . . ." she shouted in one prolonged burst of hysterics and ran into the bedroom.

Ralph must have been listening closely, for no sooner had she mentioned the word "police" than he came tumbling down the stairs on his stumpy legs. He looked terribly solemn. He put his hand on my shoulder and began leading me towards the door.

"Go home quickly, Tristan, or she'll get the police on us."

"For what? What have I done? I did exactly as you told me."

"Yes, yes, but you shouldn't have done what I told you. It's gone too far now."

"What's gone too far? I don't know what you are talking about, Ralph. Will you explain . . ."

"Another time. You buzz off now."

"Buzz off! Am I not then to move in with you? Only yesterday you said I could stay with you till death do us part."

"Tristan, if you don't leave soon enough, she'll phone the police. Do you understand—the police. The bully boys in the uniforms!"

"What can the police do? It's a domestic affair."

"What can the police do? I'll tell you, but first you get out of the house."

He pushed me out and then stepped out himself. He closed the door with a bang. "This is to let Maura know you are out," he said, and went on, "The bitch once got the police down to say that I was harassing her and would they throw me out. They asked me who I was and I said I was her husband. She said no, and I had one hell of a time proving that I was. They wanted to see my marriage certificate, and I turned the house upside-down before I could find it. Just when I had satisfied the police, she sneaked on me: said I smoked hash—kept it in my mattress. The guys took my mattress away and for six weeks I slept on the floor till I bought myself another mattress from a garage sale. I don't want the police here—not by a long way."

I reminded Ralph of all the nice things he had said about Maura: that she was kind, noble, generous, and would make me an excellent wife. He said he took it all back now and I should forget her—she wasn't good enough for me, just as she wasn't good enough for him. I told him that I could never forget Maura after all the love and joy we had shared. Even if I did forget her, I could never forget Clare. And for him to ask me to forget Clare would be a sacrilege. He thought for a while, and said, "Tristan, you can see Clare. I see a way. . ."

"How?" I interrupted him, unable to contain my joy. "Ralph, if I can see Clare even once a week, I'm prepared to forget Maura completely."

"When Maura goes out, I'll bring Clare over to your apartment. When she's out for a short time, she leaves the kid with me."

"God bless you, Ralph," I cried. "You have given me more than any woman has ever given me. Ask for whatever you want—anything, anything I can do for you."

Always keep a dozen beers chilled and ready in your fridge. You can never tell when I'll drop in with Clare. While you give her suck, I can wet my lips."

I stretched out my hand to him in gratitude, but he refused to take it. He said Maura might be spying on us from the window and if she saw him shaking hands with me she'd imagine we had hatched up a plot. In fact it would be better if Maura saw him kick my ass—it would put her off the scent completely. I told him I wouldn't agree to such an indignity. He assured me that the kick he had in mind was only "symbolic" and that I wouldn't have to bend over to receive it. For Clare's sake I agreed, and true to his word Ralph landed a soft one on my backside.

I drove away—not too unhappy.

16

"You're looking pretty good," said Enright, putting his hand on my shoulder and directing me towards his office.

I was bright enough this morning to see that he had on his mind something else besides my good looks, and I was quick enough to take the opportunity his remarks provided.

"I'm also *feeling* pretty good, doctor. I think you've sent for me to tell me I can now resume teaching."

"Not exactly, Tristan."

"I can't think of anything else. The fall semester is not too far off."

"How are your breasts?"

"Maura and I are having problems. Our future depends very much on my getting back my job."

"Maura came to see me yesterday."

"When?"

"I think it was soon after you saw her. She's very disturbed and wants to be left alone. I told her I'd talk to you. What's the matter?"

I told Enright everything that had happened to me in the past two days: starting with the miscarriage on my birthday, the appearance of Martell, the refuge I took in Ralph's apartment, and my final encounter with Maura while Martell was visiting her."

"To me she seems a little unbalanced," I concluded. "I hope there's nothing seriously wrong with her."

Enright ignored my remarks. "You'll recall that I tried to discourage you in the beginning from seeing her," he said.

"You did say she was not good enough for me, and yesterday Ralph said much the same thing."

"I did not say she was not good enough for you! I might have said you two are not good for each other."

"That comes to the same thing."

"No, it doesn't. Anyway, that's not what I called you for. Maura does not want to have anything to do with you, and I personally feel you'd be better off without her."

"How would I be better off?"

Enright didn't know what to say. He began fumbling for words—no doubt a consequence of not following his own advice to his patients: think before you open your mouth.

"Doctor, I love Maura and I'll do anything for her happiness," I said to help him out. As I liked the sound of my pledge, I repeated the words again.

"Then forget her. Leave the woman alone."

"You are asking for too much. Even if I do forget her, I may not be able to leave her alone."

As Enright didn't understand what I meant, I explained to him my deep attachment to Clare and how I would have to force my way into Maura's house to see Clare if Ralph failed to bring her periodically to my place. He was greatly perturbed by my new friendship with Ralph and the deal I had struck with him. He began referring to my love for Clare as "unnatural," quite forgetting that he himself had recommended the breast shield. He argued that if I could give up the mother, I could certainly give up the child. I told him there was a great difference, both physically and mentally, between the mother and the child and I was prepared to elaborate on it. He said there was no need—he knew the difference. It then occurred to me that this was the time to find out if his estimation of Clare agreed with mine.

"Doctor, do you think Clare is an extraordinary being?"

"I don't know what you mean by extraordinary. She is, from what I can see, a normal child. Maura suspects she is a bit retarded, but with children one cannot say for sure until they are two or three years old."

"The bloody bitch. How dare she call my darling retarded!"

"Tristan!"

"I'm sorry, doctor, but I too know something about children. Clare is . . ."

"Yes, what is she?" he asked as I checked myself, realizing that he lacked my breadth of vision.

"Let it be. Time will show and, God willing, in our lifetime."

Enright didn't ask me to elucidate; he seemed quite ready to wait and see. This lack of curiosity is a serious failing in this doctor, but I have stayed on with him since I need little medical attention and he is genuinely sympathetic towards me.

"I want to help you, Tristan," he said. "I want you to give up Maura and Clare."

"I can't."

"But you must."

"How? Tell me how?"

"Share your love with others."

I told him I was prepared to share Clare without any hesitation, for she had a marked preference for my nipples and was thoroughly reliable. But I couldn't say the same about Maura. Still, I was prepared to try if there was no other remedy in sight. If I must share her, I'd rather share her with him than anyone else, and I hoped he wouldn't mind my standing by and holding his bifocals while Maura rode him. He shook his head several times and said I had got him all wrong. By sharing he meant that I should not expend all my love on Maura and Clare alone, but bestow it liberally on other women and children. He concluded by comparing my love to pollution—dangerous in its concentrated form, but relatively harmless when diffused or absorbed into the atmosphere.

17

"Come one, come all," I said, getting up on the pedestal at the Speakers' Corner. "Suffer little children, and forbid them not, to come unto me: for of such is the kingdom of heaven." And I let go of a balloon from the two score or more tied to my wrist. The children looked heaven-wards, all save one.

"Rise up ye women that are at ease, and give ear unto my speech. Rise up, ye happy ones, ye fruitful ones, ye whom the Lord hath blessed." And I let go another balloon as I beckoned the pregnant women with wide gestures of my arms.

A dozen kids between three and six left their play and followed me, laughing, skipping, calling me "mister, mister, mister." An equal number of women heaved themselves out of garden chairs and waddled towards me like Canada geese quack-quacking. Their loose shirts fell over the contours of their beautifully rounded bellies, and I wished I could sneak into one of them and be a child again.

It is a small and devout crowd that I gather now. But you should have seen the crowd I collected when I first started speaking some three weeks ago. On the first day the entire park turned out to hear me—five hundred people, if not more. From the way they heckled and abused me, you would have thought I was on the brink of a political career. I told the audience that I was not interested in politics and sought no honour and glory for myself, but love for these little children and the mothers who bore them. Still, tomatoes and eggs (not rotten ones) were thrown at me, and one from the crowd called me a pedophile. I was about to bring down the wrath of God on him when I was distracted by a woman who had got hold of her son by his shirt tail and was bawling at him, "You mustn't go near a stranger."

"Stranger?" I asked with a benevolent smile. "Mother, Jesus was also a stranger and still is to a few hardened hearts."

"He's a nut," coughed an old-age pensioner. "This goddamn country is full of them."

Ignoring him, I continued, "Mother, your boy's father too was a stranger until you met him. Let us break this barrier, let us love and share our love."

"Don't call me 'mother', you maniac," the woman yelled at me.

With a poise which must have been heaven's gift to me, for I had not seen it in myself before, I said, "I am your son, whatever you may call me. We are all your children, young and old. Every woman, however ugly or depraved she may be, still partakes of the Universal Mother—the Mother of God."

Stirring as my words were, they did not impress this mother of God, who left, muttering a curse. But many of the other women in the crowd gave each other significant looks and nodded assent to my pronouncement.

By the third day the crowd had begun to dwindle. On the fourth day a reporter from *The Hemisphere*, who once happened to be a none-too-bright student of mine, gave me a half-page coverage along with a three-column photograph. The photograph showed me standing on the pedestal holding balloons. But that day I had donned a mortarboard to ward off the hot August sun, and I dare say I looked a little like the College Vice-Chancellor himself. But this ill-informed reporter, more anxious to boost Canada's image abroad than speak the truth, began by comparing me with Guru Maharaj Ji. "Could Tristan Ediott [*sic*] be the new Guru?" he asked in the caption to the photograph. Thank God he misspelled my name. It saved me not only from numerous telephone calls from my admirers, but also from the envy of my colleagues. For to get into the local paper is a sure sign that you have served the community and deserve a special increase in salary.

This reporter pointed out that the United States' Guru Maharaj Ji has several titles such as Perfect Master, Lord of the Universe, Saviour of Mankind, Revealer of Light, Peace, Love, Unity and everything Eternal. He also owns cars, airplanes and homes around the world. But Canada's Guru has only an MA from a Midlands university and has now been pensioned off by his College (a gross misstatement; I am not pensioned off—I am on salary continuance insurance like several distinguished members of the faculty). He then tried to be clever and said that "Dr [*sic*] Elliott's message of sharing love, which he initially got from his doctor who shall remain nameless, is bogged with insurmountable difficulties." But he did not say what these difficulties were and why they should be insurmountable! And he made no mention of several other topics on which I speak with considerable knowledge and experience.

However, the newspaper coverage brought me a fresh crowd for the next two days. But their minds had already been poisoned by the words "insurmountable difficulties" and they could not understand my doctrine of sharing love. One man felt that mine was an invidious plan to seduce other people's wives, and he said so bluntly. Nothing could have been more foreign to my mind. I stood aghast. I was so shocked that I could not utter a single word in my own defence. Many took my silence as an admission of guilt and left me. But a few remained—the faithful few who now stood before me and who, I know, will be with me forever. They occasionally joke and laugh at me and think I am funny. I don't mind it as long as I have their love.

"Kids, today I am going to speak to your mothers on a delicate subject. So you can have your balloons and go and play." I should mention here that I speak in the Biblical style only when I am opening or ending a discourse; the rest of the time I speak plain English.

"Mister, what about giving us some candies?" asked a

youngster.

"You'll have some tomorrow."

"'You said so yesterday, mister. You said we'd have candies today."

"Did I? Then I have lied. Tomorrow I am going to tell you the story of Jacob and what happened to him when he lied to his father, Isaac."

"Mister, before we go, could you give us a ride?"

I occasionally give the children a ride. I go down on my hands and knees and imitate a horse, a camel or a donkey. I hold a ribbon between my teeth, and the kid riding me pulls at the two ends of the ribbon as if it were a reign. This has given me a sore mouth. The last time I was a horse a girl kicked me with her heels in the stomach to make me go faster. I had a bellyache, and I don't relish giving rides anymore. But the children love it and, give and take a little, I prefer it to Maura riding me.

"You can all ride me tomorrow if you go away now. I have something urgent to say to the mothers and then I have to go and meet an important man. If this man keeps his promise, then I shall have a lot of money and I'll buy you fruits and milk. Candies are bad for your teeth and they give you diabetes."

"What's diabetes, mister?" asked another kid.

"Now scamp off if you want goodies tomorrow."

The children left with the balloons, all except Lianne. Lianne is the little girl who didn't look heavenwards when I let go the first balloon.

Lianne is about five, with a small red mouth and large blue eyes. She has not missed a day since I began speaking; she is always the first to come and the last to leave. She does not mix with the other kids, but stands a little distance away from them, her eyes riveted on me. She never laughs or talks, or looks at the birds and clouds as other children do. She does not tug at my clothes to draw my attention when I am distributing candy or balloons. She accepts a gift only when I call her by name, and she quickly returns to her spot with a curt "thank you" to fix her relentless gaze on me.

I let Lianne stay—I liked her more than the other kids. Besides she is not really a kid. What she is I really don't know. But I know she is studying me and she has something important to say. She will say it to me when the time comes.

"Mothers," I began, "on the last occasion I spoke to you on diarrhea. Today I'm . . ."

"Before that you spoke on bowel movement, constipation, enemas and suppositories," interrupted Edna. She has five kids and is forever knitting socks.

All the women laughed. I couldn't understand why.

"I did so, mothers," I said. "Why do you laugh?"

"Go on, go on, Tristan," said Valerie, who sat next to Edna. "Pay no attention to her."

"Well," I continued, "today I am going to speak on diaper rashes. I asked the children to leave not because the subject concerns their private parts, but because I don't want them to know that this horrible and persistent disease was inflicted on them by their parents., For that would turn their innocent minds against the very people who brought them into this world."

"How did we give them the rash?" asked Edna.

"You gave them the rash by not giving them enough of your love; by not changing their diapers every time they passed water. This water, for I hate to use the ugly word 'urine' for what these lovely kids make, has in it a bacterium called 'ammoniagenes' which produces ammonia. The ammonia . . ."

Edna interrupted me again. "Tristan, did you ever have diaper rash?"

I was trying to remember if I had, when Jean came to my rescue. "He didn't! In India they don't have food, leave alone diapers."

"She is right, mother. Diaper rashes are God's curse on the affluent. But why should the little children suffer for the sins of their parents?"

"Come on, Tristan. Diaper rash isn't that serious," said Valerie. "It is one of the many things a kid has to go through in his first two years."

"He needn't," is what I was about to say when something strange happened to me—something that has never happened before. All of a sudden it got dark and I saw a vast concourse of children sucking at their mothers' breasts. They all looked alike: black, potbellied, their arms and legs thin as reeds. Then, like a well-rehearsed drill, they all at once left their mother's breasts and turned their gaze on me. These children had no mouths; there was nothing in their faces save the whites of their eyes.

I narrated my vision to the mothers and asked them what it could mean. They all had worried looks on their faces except Edna. She said I was suffering from malnutrition.

"Where do you have your meals?" she asked. "Do you cook for yourself?"

"I live on cheese and crackers, mother."

"Ah, you need better nourishment than that. You need a woman to look after you." And turning to Valerie, she asked, "Why don't you take in this poor guy as a boarder?"

Before Valerie could open her mouth, I said I didn't need anyone to look after me, that if they had any love in their hearts they should pay heed to my words and make their little ones happier. I then begged them not to interrupt me for I had a lot to say and time was running out. They agreed, and I told them everything about diapers: the fabric they should be made from, the way they should be washed, dried, folded and pinned. I then descended the pedestal with a word of warning to the mothers: "But whoso shall offend one of these little ones which believeth in me, it were better for him that a millstone were hanged about his neck, and that he were drowned in the depths of the sea."

"Three cheers for Tristan; hip, hip, hurray!" called Edna, waving a half-knit sock.

"Hip, hip hurray!" cried all, except Lianne.

At the park gate I turned round. Tiny drops of rain were coming down and the mothers were running for shelter. Lianne, alone, was still standing—looking in my direction.

18

I arrived ten minutes before two and was immediately shown into Peabody's office by Miss Mortimer. Peabody wasn't visible at first: he was sunk deep in an enormous recliner facing the other way, and all I could see were his feet sticking in the air. I went round to face him. He looked resplendent in his doctoral gown, but most of him was hidden under a huge volume which happened to be his COLLECTED WORKS—unpublished.

"How are you,sir?"

"I've been meditating the thankless Muse." And he intoned in his husky voice:

Alas! What boots it with uncessant care
To tend the homely, slighted, shepherd's trade,
And strictly meditate the thankless Muse?

"Who wrote those lines?" he asked.

"You, sir."

"Not quite," he said with a complacent smile. "It's Milton. The shepherd's trade, Tristan, is not something one chooses; one is chosen by it. I must, perforce, return to the shepherd's trade."

As I didn't know what to say, I looked down. On the floor were empty cardboard cartons. What were they doing here? He must have read my thought, for he said, "These boxes have been here for two weeks. If they had lips they would say, 'Fill thou me to the brim.' My ultimatum to the Dean expires at 5 p.m. today, but I'm giving him two more days to reverse his decision. The Administration here is like a fickle woman who cannot make up her mind. And I hate packing and unpacking."

"What's happening, sir?"

"Happening! You are not going to tell me you don't know what's happening?"

"How would I know? The last time I was here you said you'd speak to the Dean about me. When Miss Mortimer phoned me this morning, I thought you might have some good news for me."

Peabody sighed, and shook his head. "I have some bad news and not for you alone. The very existence of the Department is in jeopardy."

"What! Has the enrollment fallen?"

"The enrollment has gone up since I took over as Acting Chairman. But I'm stepping down."

"Impossible! The election, sir! Aren't you going to fight the election?"

"Tristan, I'd fight Satan himself if he met me face to face."

"Sir, I don't understand—I don't understand at all."

With my help Peabody got out of the recliner into which he had sunk even deeper. He sat behind his desk and told me all that had transpired since I last saw him, and I could not help admiring the man's courage and uprightness. The wily Dunlop, realizing that he could not win against Peabody, had asked for a year's leave of absence on medical grounds and a postponement of the elections until next September. The Dean had unfortunately agreed to both requests and asked Peabody to continue as Acting Chairman.

"I've told the Dean that the election must take place as scheduled. The Department cannot wait till 'Caesar's wife shall have better dreams'."

"You have my vote, sir."

"It's more than your vote I need now. There may be no voting. I have refused to serve as Acting Chairman, and the Dean has decided to bring a Chairman from outside. Do you see the implication of this?"

"By golly, I do. You won't be Chairman any longer."

"No, no, that's not important. Though the job rightly belongs to me. I've given the best months of my life to it, and the Department has shown its gratitude by already arranging a farewell party for me."

"Why didn't I get an invitation?"

"I have asked my colleagues to desist, for a party would sound the death knell of the Department. It is to save the Department that I've sent for you. Don't you see how the Dean's decision to get a man from outside affects you?"

I tried hard, but I couldn't. I wanted to impress Peabody, but today I wasn't at my brightest. I admitted defeat.

"Your inability to see beneath the Dean's motive enhances my respect for you. It shows that you are a scholar, not a contriver. You know, when I joined the academic community I thought I'd be freed from the intrigues and machinations one finds in other professions. I didn't know that these vices would follow me to the very slopes of Parnassus."

Peabody explained to me the consequences of the Dean's decision and how it would affect me personally. If the Dean brought a Chairman from outside, he would have to offer him a permanent position. But the Department was already overstaffed and there were no vacancies. The only position he could offer would be mine since I hadn't been teaching for two years.

"Blast him, but I'm a tenured member of the Faculty. I can't be dismissed." And I brought my fist down on the table with a force which made Peabody jump.

"Reserve your righteous indignation for the Dean, Tristan. I'm on your side."

"When do I see the Dean?" I asked, standing up.

"Sit down, Tristan. There are a few things I'd like to know. When can you resume teaching?"

"Right now—this very minute."

"Is your doctor willing to certify that you can teach?"

"My doctor! The last time you said you didn't need a certificate from my doctor—that you could judge things for yourself."

I must have spoken with some irritation, for Peabody lost his temper and lashed out at me.

"Tristan! Mind your manners; I won't have you speak to me in this way. I know what I said and I don't need to be reminded by you. I can make up my mind, but the Dean might want something from your doctor."

"I'm sorry, sir."

"I'm doing everything I can to help you," he said, calming down a little. "The least you can do is show a sense of gratitude. For your sake I even extended the deadline of my ultimatum to the Dean."

"I apologize, sir. I will always remain your debtor. I wish there were more people like you in the world."

"That's all right. The present business has put us all under a strain. Now, I want you to conduct your negotiations with the Dean very carefully. Be firm, be precise. Don't volunteer any information on your own. Don't say I have asked you to see him. Simply tell him that you wish to resume teaching and that you have discussed it with your doctor. Tristan, have you discussed the matter with your doctor?"

"I did mention to my doctor I want to resume teaching."

"What did he say?'

"H said I could wait a little longer."

"Well, that's a discussion. It is quite safe to say you have 'discussed it.' There is no lie in that. But don't tell him what your doctor said. Even if you can join the Department in January, the Dean will find it difficult to fill your position."

"Sir, should I tell him I am a tenured member?"

"By all means. Remind him that you are a tenured member and according to the Collective Agreement the College has signed with the Faculty Association your services cannot be terminated."

"I'll do that."

"Ask him if he is bringing in a new Chairman. If he says yes, tell him that the entire Department is solidly behind Dr Peabody and will not stand for an outsider.

"Anything more, sir?"

"Just this: don't be awed by the Dean. He's a bully. Don't let him bully you. Remember, your MA is superior to his."

"Is that so? He is from Oxford."

"His is a bought degree! And he paid less for it than you would now pay for a decent meal in Erigon."

"I'll remember that."

"No, forget it. You are going to the Dean to make a case for yourself—not to examine his credentials."

"Right, sir."

"The Dean should be in his office. Go and tell his secretary you have something urgent to discuss with him."

Peabody got up and accompanied me to the elevator. "Good luck, and God be with you," he said as I pressed the button for the fifth floor.

The Dean was sitting at his desk, stroking his beard and looking distractedly at the clutter of files, letters and papers in front of him. He was colourless; he was like an artist's sketch of a man wanted for questioning by the police.

"What is this urgent business?" he asked in a tired voice.

"I wish to resume my teaching duties," I said. I wanted to tell him I was perfectly fit now, but I remembered Peabody's advice not to volunteer any information on my own.

He made no answer, but began going through the mess on his table. Finally he found what he was looking for. It was a copy of *The Hemisphere*, showing me wearing a mortarboard and holding balloons.

"What have you to say to this?" he asked, leaning over his desk to pass the paper over to me.

I took the paper, looked at my photograph, and returned it to him. "I can do better than that with my Brownie," I said.

"What?"

"The photographer should have used a filter. The sun was

too bright and therefore you see those shadows on the left."

"Is that all you have to say?"

"Yes. And it was taken without my consent."

"This picture is a disgrace to the entire faculty."

"Since when has service to the community been a disgrace?" I asked sternly, recalling Peabody's warning that the Dean is a bully. "The *Faculty Handbook* clearly lists public service as one of the criteria for advancement."

"What advancement?"

"Promotions. But I have not come to ask for a promotion. I only want to resume my teaching duties."

"Whether you can teach or not is a matter I must leave to your new Chairman to decide."

"New Chairman! Who's the new Chairman?"

The Dean did not reply, and I took the opportunity to caution him that the entire Department stood solidly behind Peabody and would not accept a man from outside. He raised his eyebrows and asked me where I got my information from.

As I ducked the question, he said he had received several phone calls from the Department members requesting a new Chairman. This floored me completely, and when I gathered my wits again I was concerned primarily with my future and nothing else.

"Sir, I hope the man you are hiring is not being considered for my slot. I have academic tenure and I plan to stay here."

"Tristan, I sympathize with you and I am concerned about you, but we cannot keep you on the Faculty indefinitely. You have not taught for two years, and as I see it you are not in a condition to teach in the foreseeable future."

"What am I to do then?"

"Nothing. As long as you are sick you are safe—the salary continuance insurance will take care of you. It's only the healthy who have to face unemployment."

"Sir, may I draw your attention to the Collective Agreement. A tenured faculty member can only be dismissed for gross misconduct and nothing else."

"Employment can be terminated if the person is unfit to perform his duties."

"Yes. But the Agreement specifies that in all such cases the person should be retrained and rehired in another capacity. I am prepared to be retrained."

"Retrained!" And he picked up *The Hemisphere* and threw it at me. "Look at that again, man. Retrain you for what? A circus?"

I looked intently at my photograph. I had a brain wave. I jumped up and said, "Day care. Retrain me for the College Day Care. I want to work in the Day Care."

The Dean looked with relieved amazement. "That's a possibility," he said wistfully, half to himself and half to me. "Tristan, you get in touch with me again in December."

While making my exit, I turned round to thank him. He was smiling, shaking his head, and musing, "Tristan William Elliott, Assistant Professor of Day Care."

I was pleased he was taking care of my academic rank without my having to ask. Not that I am fussy about it.

19

In a way I'm glad I am not teaching—I wouldn't know where to fit in my classes. I have a tight schedule. In the morning I go to the Safeway. Maura does her shopping there and I get a chance to see Clare as she is wheeled about in a grocery cart. I have to be careful though, for if Maura found me watching Clare she would scream me out of the store. At midday I am in the park to speak to the mothers and the children. Around three I go to the Public Library to weed out books unfit for the perusal of kids and I put these stealthily on shelves beyond their reach. Henry Miller with his obsession for "everything that flows" is a particular hazard. From the library I go to the Regency Clinic to sit in the waiting-room and meditate on the pregnant women who come to visit their doctors. To me there is nothing more edifying than the sight of a woman in her final months of pregnancy. On weekends, when the clinic is shut, I crisscross the maternity wards of the General Hospital. If a nurse looks suspiciously at me, I go up to her and ask, "In which ward is Elsa Elliott?" I nearly fainted the other day when a nurse answered crisply, "Ward B4." I return home at seven. Ralph drops in with Clare every second or third evening, for Maura is still high on Women's Lib. Before going to bed I choose a story from the Bible for the kids and prepare my next day's discourse for the mothers. I have the finest collection of paperbacks on childbirth and child care, though a few of the questions the mothers ask require divine guidance. Valerie wanted to know why older women run the risk of giving birth to a mongoloid. I prayed for several hours before I got the answer. It was God's way of saying that infancy is blessed, and that the older we grow the more stupid we become till in the end it affects our progeny.

I came home early today. I was forced to abandon my discourse, for no sooner had I begun than the Shriners appeared with their band. They were men mostly in their fifties and sixties. They wore fezzes and fancy costumes and looked like characters from *Ali Baba and the Forty Thieves*. The way they pranced and leaped would have made a cow laugh. I recognized my Dean: he was the youngest of the lot and cut a caper higher than the others. As I stood helpless, my devotees moved away until I was left alone with little Lianne. I asked her if she would now tell me what she had to say. She opened her mouth as if to speak, but made no sound. Then, like the rest of them, she too turned and left.

I lay on my bed thinking of Lianne. Was she alone like me, or did she have any brothers and sisters? And parents? And what did they do? Soon my thoughts drifted to my widowed mother in India, and I began to feel guilty for not having written to her all these months. My mother! My beautiful mother who wrote in every letter, "Dear Child, How I long to be with you. I hope you will come back soon." First the letters came every week. Then at intervals of fifteen days. Then the intervals grew to a month, two months, three months. And now? I hadn't heard from her for a long time, but were I to get a letter tomorrow it would say the same thing. I couldn't go back to my mother but I could call her here. She'd be proud to hear my discourses, proud that the love she gave me I have passed on to others.

I was writing to my mother when the phone rang. It was Ralph wanting to know if he could bring Clare over.

"Now?" I asked.

"Brother, I need to get out, it's been one hell of a morning. Martell dropped in early to take away his priceless black moon—Enright offered him a hundred bucks for it. But Maura wouldn't let it go; said she'd buy it herself. She asked me for a loan. Now you know I have no money. I told her so. She began abusing me, calling me names, bum, bastard, anything she could think of. Then she began crying. Martell tried to comfort her, but he too began crying. And Clare—she joined in too."

"You mean they made my Clare cry!" I said boiling over with rage.

"They did. They made your poor child cry."

"The swines! Where are they now?"

"Martell has taken her out for lunch. He agreed to let her keep the painting. While they were going out, I heard Maura say "Foul Play" between sobs. I think she's thinking of the movie, unless she means Enright. Tristan, you've never taken me to a movie. I want to see *The Yum-Yum Girls*."

I asked Ralph to give me fifteen minutes. I then ran to the corner store and got a jar of Marmite. Clare has become very choosy and won't even sniff at my nipples unless I apply something delectable. My fridge is filled with jams of every kind, but lately she has developed a taste for Marmite. And as it is sticky, she sucks longer, and gets more satisfaction. And so do I.

When giving suck to Clare I take off my shirt and vest and cover myself with a bedsheet. The clothes get in the way of Clare moving from one breast to another; besides Marmite stains are hard to remove. Also, I have two shirts left. Once I get the day care job, I'll be able to afford a proper wardrobe.

Ralph today made an unusual request while I was giving suck to Clare.

"Aye, Tristan, show us your tits," he said.

"No."

"Come, don't be shy. What's there in a man's tits? You can see mine!"

"I don't want to."

"By God, you've seen mine. You saw it the day Maura threw you out. And you saw something more!"

"I didn't want to."

"OK, Tristan, have it your way. I still see no harm in your

showing me your tits. I only wanted to see if they were like Maura's. But I guess any tits would be bigger than hers."

"Could we change the subject?"

Ralph nodded. He sat thinking for a while and then shook his head. He got up and went to the fridge and pulled out two bottles of Molson's beer.

"Tristan, why do you always buy Canadian beer? Is it to support the ind . . . indi . . . ? Hell! I can't get the word. But you know what I mean."

"Indigenous?"

"That's the word. Indigenous industry."

He looked at me, but I looked the other way. He continued, uncapping the bottles:

"I like foreign beer: Heineken from Holland and Tuborg from Denmark. They are low-caloried and good for the heart. You live longer if you take care of your health. And I want to live till Clare grows up. Once she has a boyfriend who can take care of her, I can call it quits."

"Foreign beer costs twice as much," I observed.

"I know it. But think of Clare. If you buy me Tuborg, you buy it for Clare. After all, I'm her dad. No better way of showing love to a child than by prolonging the life of the father!"

"Ralph, Maura told me you said Clare is not your child."

"She's a crazy bitch. You see I didn't want to have a child. You can't fuck a pregnant woman the way . . ."

"Please," I interrupted.

"Sorry, brother, I forgot. You can't have 'religious liaison' with a pregnant woman the way you can with others. So I took every precaution. But, Christ, she beat me."

I asked him how. He said Maura wanted a child badly and stopped taking the pill. But he began wearing "the hat" (as he put it) every time he made love to her. When she got pregnant, it baffled him and he swore the child was somebody else's. At this time Maura was seeing a Mexican who worked in her office. His name was Señor something—he could never remember what. So he said it was the Señor's baby. But Maura proved that it was his.

"How did she prove it?" I asked.

"When I told Maura that I'd been using the rubber and the baby couldn't be mine, she said she'd cut the tips off the six dozen rubbers I had bought at a sale. I looked at the rubbers I kept under the mattress and, damn it, she had done it. I had been flooding her all the while without knowing that I was leaking. Now that's what I call mean, Tristan."

"Was she always like that?"

"Hell, no. She was a fine woman when I married her. She used to cook for me, wash for me, adore me.When I came home in the evening she'd welcome me with a bottle of beer. While I sat and relaxed she'd take off my shoes and bring my slippers. She'd sit in my lap and put her head on my chest and say the most loving things to me. She'd cook me a royal dinner and after I had eaten I'd take her to bed. I 'liaisoned' her every night—period or no period. I was her lord and master and she was my slave. It was the happiest time of my life. The only thing I didn't like about her was that she was skinny and had a very small ass. But so what—the woman was mine. You can't have everything perfect, can you?"

"No, but what went wrong?"

Ralph got up and fetched himself another beer. He held the bottle at arms length and, fixing his gaze on it, said:

"Drink will destroy me if I don't master it."

"How do you master it?"

"By drinking more and more till you develop stamina. I don't believe in fleeing from evil, I conquer it—be it indi . . . indigenous or foreign."

"You were going to tell me what went wrong between you and Maura," I reminded him.

"The Women's Lib. Roxanne and Vanessa and the whole bloody lot of them. They ruined her. She forgot her religion, she forgot the Bible. She wanted her rights! The home went to the dogs! I went to the dogs! If only I could meet Roxanne when she's alone I'd rape her."

"Knowing her, I wouldn't pray for that! Besides they owe the Women's Lib to us. If we hadn't exploited women, there'd be no Lib."

"What do you mean?"

"Why shouldn't they be paid equal salaries for equal work?"

"Equal work! By God, Tristan! What work has Maura done since she joined the Lib, save ride you and me?"

"She worked for the newspaper."

"Worked! My ass! She wrote more letters to the editor than she typed for him. In the evenings she would sit with her 'sisters' and jabber about spreading the 'gospel' from Peru to Papua New Guinea. No more breakfast for me, no more dinners. She started learning karate for self-defence—kicked me in the balls when my dinky was up. That was her way of saying 'not today'."

I saw no good in arguing with Ralph. I didn't want a fight with him over Maura or the Women's Lib. They meant nothing to me now. All I wanted was to be with Clare, and Ralph had come as a saviour. What would I have done without him? I turned to look at Clare as she played quietly by herself on the floor.

"Whatever Maura may be, she has given you a lovely kid. You can be proud of her, Ralph."

"Isn't she lovely," he said looking at Clare. "Just like her father. I wish, though, she had a better mother. If only you could have been her mother, Tristan, this girl would have had a future. I do my best for her. I work and slog the whole day and spend every penny I have on her. But a child needs a mother just as much as it needs a father."

"That's true."

"Tristan, you have a son. Does he have a father? I mean a sort of father you are to Clare?"

I told Ralph what I told Maura: that I had married Elsa on the rebound and that I detested her. But my initial detestation of her, I said, was nothing compared to what it was now, for she had deprived me of my son by fleeing to Germany. My boy was growing up without the loving care of a father. I wished she would marry and give the boy a father. But I saw little hope, for who would marry 180 pounds?

"What was that? Say it again, Tristan."

"She weighs 180 pounds."

"You're kidding."

"I'm not. I weighed her."

"Bless you, brother. That's marvellous. I have always wanted a woman with some meat on her. Maura bruises me all over with her bones. Why not call Elsa here. I'll marry her. And you know I'll be a good father to your boy. "

I couldn't help smiling at the thought of him and Elsa together. Funny as it seemed I couldn't impose Elsa on a friend who had been good to me. Ralph had his failings, no doubt, but they were not because he lacked character, but because he lacked education. Had he gone to Leeds like me, he too would have been different. He was too direct and forthright and did not know the right terminology for many of the things he said. I told him that I wasn't in communication with Elsa and didn't even know where she lived. His face fell, and I felt sorry I couldn't help him.

"Is there anything else I can do for you?" I asked.

"Ya, I want a woman."

"You'll find one. What about the girl I once saw with you?"

""I don't want a western woman. I want love, I want affection, I want a poke," he said sorrowfully.

He looked terribly dejected and I felt unhappy that I could do nothing about it. I tried to sympathize with him.

"I know how you feel, Ralph. If I knew a girl I would introduce her to you."

Suddenly his face brightened. He stood up and did the twist.

"Aye, Tristan, I have an idea. You get me a woman from India. I want an Indian woman. I want to be loved. I want to be worshipped. I want a home."

"I hope you also want children, Ralph."

"Nope. Not unless you want to give them suck."

"I do."

"You get me a wife from India and I'll give you children—as many as you want. When do you get me a wife?"

To humour him I said I'd get him one when I went to India. He now wanted me to go to India as soon as possible.

"Why not go next week?" he asked. "I'll drive you to the airport; it will save you a couple of bucks."

"Thanks for the offer, but I can't leave Clare and go," I said.

"You go when Maura goes to Chicago."

"What?"

"She wants to study Women Power. They have a school there."

"When is she going?" It had never crossed my mind that Maura might one day leave and I would be left without Clare. I couldn't do without Clare—I'd go raving mad.

Ralph must have sensed my fear, for he began to comfort me. He said Maura is always talking about going, but who knows if she ever will. Even if she did go, it would be only for six weeks—it's a short course and they have a long waiting list. And if she stays any longer than six weeks, he'll himself go down to Chicago to fetch Clare for me.

"You promise me you'll fetch Clare," I asked.

"Promise. But you'll have to find me a wife."

"Done. I'll have to get you one from here. I'm not going to India."

I thought I'd be able to persuade one of the separated or divorced mothers to accept Ralph. The mothers have great respect for me and will do whatever I tell them.

"I'd have preferred an Indian, but I suppose I'll take what I get. I'm hungry for love. Later when you go to India you could get me one from there as well."

"All right, Ralph," I said looking at my watch. "Shouldn't you be on your way now?"

He asked me what time it was. I told him it was close to five.

"My God!" he gasped. "The bitch will put me through a cross-examination and I'm no good at lying." And he got hold of Clare and bolted from the room.

"Let me kiss Clare goodbye," I called running after him.

But he was gone. Holding Clare on his shoulders with both hands, he was going down the stairs with the force of a baseball. From the landing of the third floor he bellowed at me, "Don't forget your promise. Ask her if she'd like to see *The Yum-Yum Girls* with me."

20

Things are not going too well with me, but I have great hopes for tomorrow.

This morning Peabody phoned me to say a new Chairman has been appointed, but his own services to the Department have been suitably recognized and he has been appointed Chairman Emeritus. I congratulated him and asked him what happens to me now. He said he sympathized with me, but he couldn't use his exalted office to buy favours. And last evening Ralph turned up, not with Clare but with a whore. He drank a dozen bottles of my beer and then took the woman into my bedroom. When the two left, I found my bed soiled and I had to sleep on the sofa. What else was in store for me? I asked myself as I got into my car.

On the way to the park, I stopped at a toyshop to buy balloons for the kids. I saw Martell in tattered dungarees standing on a stool and painting a blue circle on the front wall of the shop. The circle grew bigger each time he dipped his brush into a bucket of paint. I wondered why the owner would want a moon on the wall.

"Martell, what the hell are you doing?"

"Tristan!" he called out gleefully stepping down from the stool and embracing me fulsomely so that some of the paint from his dungarees got onto my clothes.

"You're not painting a moon, are you?"

"I've given up painting moons. There is no future in it. I've become a house painter now. " And he brought his face close to my ear and whispered, "There's good money in it—I insist on minimum wages."

"But that looks so much like a moon!"

"Old habits die hard, Tristan. When this circle touches the top and bottom edges of the wall and can grow no bigger, I'll stop and fill in the four corners. After the job's finished, it will look like any other wall. But, boy, there'll be a moon in it—just like the moon right now in the sky. You can't see it, but I can. The moon is indestructible—it is always there."

I thought Martell must be going through financial difficulties if he had to make a living as a house painter. I asked him if I could loan him some money.

"God, no," he said cheerfully. "I don't need money. I do it only for Maura. Poor girl, she wants to go to Chicago and needs a thousand bucks. So far I've made ninety-four."

So what Ralph said was true. It frightened me to contemplate life without Clare even for a short period, but I didn't want Martell to guess my fears. I changed the topic and asked him how things were at Kamsack.

"Grand," he said. "Boy, you left a good impression there. The doctors and nurses kept asking about you, and when they saw your picture in the newspaper, they got a bed ready for you. Every morning we bet our scrambled eggs you'd be there by evening."

I smiled. He was a loveable fool in spite of the harm he was doing me by earning money for Maura. I went into the shop after warning him not to go near Clare without washing the paint off his hands—that it contained a toxic substance which could set the child sneezing.

Back in the car with the balloons, I turned on the radio. The news was just over, and the weatherman was predicting seasonable temperatures—a sure sign that no one knew what was coming. The leaves in the park had turned yellow, and the first snow could come any day. Where would I meet the mothers and children then?

The thought set me worrying. Why hadn't it occurred to me

all these days? "I'll cross my bridges when I come to them," I said to myself as I got out of the car and walked towards the Speakers' Corner.

I climbed up the pedestal, the balloons tied to my wrist. "Come one, come all," I said as usual.

They all came.

"Mothers and children," I began.

I could not continue. Something was the matter. I searched the crowd.

"What's wrong?" I asked.

"Nothing," answered a mother.

I looked again. It wasn't what I saw every day.

"Mothers, tell me," I implored. "Don't keep me in suspense."

"Are you well, Tristan?" asked Valerie.

I looked around, frantically. I spun round and round. I saw. Lianne was not there.

"Where's Lianne?" I asked.

The mothers looked at one another.

"Where's Lianne?" I asked a little loudly.

No one would speak.

"Lianne!" I called out aloud. But there was no answer. "Lianne! Lianne!" I called in every direction. But there wasn't even an echo to my cry.

"He is sick," said Edna.

The mothers nodded. I heard words of sympathy. I also heard a titter. With my teeth I bit loose the strings that held the balloons to my wrist and sent them all to heaven.

"Mister! mister!" the children lamented as they stood with empty hands gazing at the sky.

I descended and sat down at the base of the pedestal. The mothers and children gathered round me. There was concern for me on every face.

"Please leave me alone," I said.

The mothers quietly began to move away, but not so the children. They stood staring at me with awe and fear.

"Valerie, mother, ask the kids to leave me alone," I entreated.

"Tristan, you go home," she said.

"Please," I begged.

Valerie ordered the children away. They left, not wanting to. Some walked backwards, others turned round every few steps to look at me. When they had all gone, Valerie came and put her hand on my forehead. She let it stay there for a minute.

"You don't have a fever. You'll be all right," she tried to comfort me.

I nodded.

"Is there anything I can do for you, Tristan?"

I shook my head.

She lingered for a while, unsure of what to say. Then she too left.

The mothers and children having departed, I got up to search for Lianne. As I looked distractedly at the spot where she always stood and stared at me, I didn't know where to begin. She had not left a clue I could follow up. But find her I must—I could not bear to lose any of my children.

"Lianne is gone today! Who tomorrow?" I asked.

"Clare!" the answer flashed on my mind.

A shiver ran down my spine. God had spoken. He had spoken as He always does through His silences. Lianne was God's messenger then, and those relentless eyes forever fixed on me were God's own.

Clare! I must make sure I don't lose Clare. I must take Clare away with me. But where? Where could I go? With God beside me I didn't have to think. I again saw the vision I once had: I saw a million black faces quit sucking their mothers' breasts and turn their gaze on me. But there was a difference now—they all had mouths and they were smiling and beckoning to me. And so to India. I would have preferred Bethlehem, but I go where the Lord sends me.

How I should get to India with Clare posed only a minor problem. The normal procedure of buying two tickets and checking the baggage through was out of the question. I hadn't the money for the fare and my Indian passport had long expired. As for my darling Clare, she had neither a passport nor a penny. The only course open was to rescue Clare from the Safeway while her mother shopped for the weekend, get into the car, run to my apartment, bolt the doors and ask the police for safe conduct for the two of us to India. The police would, no doubt, call it kidnapping and would do all they could to dissuade me from fulfilling my mission. But I would have to be firm. With some luck I could catch the evening plane, but I should also ready myself to hold out for a month.

Buying provisions for the siege and the trip seemed a more formidable proposition, with just four hours to go before the stores closed. There wasn't the time to prepare a list, so I decided to go to a large store and look on the shelves for the things I might need. For myself, cheese and crackers would do, but Clare would need a balanced diet.

Not wishing to take the chance of running into Maura, I hastened to the Superstore. I went straight to the section displaying baby food. As I scanned the shelves, a pretty shop assistant came up and asked if I needed any help. I was about to scoff at her offer (for who in Canada knows what's better for the baby than I do?) when I noticed she was pregnant. "Breast feed the little one when it pops out, for there is no substitute for a mother's milk," I cautioned her. She blushed and left. I then began filling my grocery basket with jars of Heinz Junior fruit salads, bananas, beef noodle, chicken noodle, turkey noodle and all other noodles. I bought cereals, bathroom tissues, Johnson's Baby Soap and Johnson's Baby Lotion. The more I bought the more confident I felt that the rescue could not fail. People fail because they often run out of provisions; sometimes they get talked into surrendering by the police, but more often they are simply worn down by lack of sleep. Above all, the vast majority of those who fail lack education. Who ever heard of a rescuer failing who was an Assistant Professor of History with an MA from Leeds to boot!

From the Superstore I drove to the Army and Navy. I bought a subaltern's uniform, a Castro cap and a cigar for myself, and a dozen white dresses for Clare. I thought of buying a gun, but I didn't want to break the law forbidding me to possess firearms. Besides, there was no one I wanted to kill. I also bought a megaphone for talking to the police and a big Pooh bear for Clare to play with. For our use in India I bought an umbrella, two life-jackets,and a plastic raincoat large enough to protect the two of us. For my mother I got some nylon stockings. After the shopping was over, I had less than a dollar left in my wallet. With that I bought some chewing gum; I find it very soothing for the nerves.

When I got back to my apartment, the sun was going down in a cloud of red. For the first time in years, I stood for a while looking at the wide expanse and the soft colours in the sky. I said "adieu" and drew the curtains. I began putting my clothes in my suitcase. I was surprised how little I possessed. Mine would not exceed the baggage limit, but would they allow little Clare her twenty kilos, I wondered. I would hate to leave behind all the food I had purchased.

Having packed my clothes, I sat down to think what else remained to be done. Nothing, except to phone in a cablegram to my mother, saying I would be arriving any day and she should keep breakfast waiting for two. She'll be glad to see Clare. She is sure to ask me if that's my boy. "No, it's God's daughter," I'll say. We'll stay in Delhi for two days. Clare will need to rest the first day, but the next day I shall take her on a sight-seeing tour of Delhi. I'll show her Humayun's Mausoleum, the Old Fort, the Red Fort, the Qutab Minar, the Supreme Court and the Presidential Palace. I must show her St. Stephen's College—my Alma Mater. It will interest her more than anything else. The following morning we shall leave by train for the holy city of Varanasi. In the train I shall tell Clare the story of Mother Ganges: how the river was once confined to the celestial regions; how it came down to the earth as a reward for the austerities observed by a sage; and how it would have flooded the earth, had not Lord Shiva allowed it to flow through his hair to break its mighty torrent. When we reach

Varanasi we shall, along with thousands of other pilgrims, bathe and purify ourselves in the crystal waters of the Ganges. We shall stand on one leg in the water and pray to God to forgive the Canadians all their sins. Then I shall buy a small sailboat. Clare will sit at the bow, dressed in a white frock with her hair done up with a red ribbon. I shall sit at the stern and steer the boat. We shall sail up-stream towards the ice-cave of Gangotri—the very source of the river eleven thousand feet high. On our way Clare will paddle her hands in the water and pick up the marigolds as they float past us. Sadhus and mahatmas in their hundreds, clad in their flowing saffron robes and their faces smeared with holy ashes, will line up the river bank. And as we sail by, they will make obeisance to Clare with joined palms.

On reaching Gangotri, we shall put up in the VIP suite of the temple while I build a small mud hut for Clare and myself. I shall plaster it with cow dung. I shall purchase a goat, and Clare will live on goat milk and fruits till she is eighteen years old. Then the two of us will descend to the plains and announce a new dispensation.

21

The excitement of being with Clare for ever was too much for me. I could not sleep a wink all night, and to steady myself I finished the remaining six bottles of beer I had bought for Ralph. When I got up from my bed in the morning I could not have been in better shape for the task that lay ahead.

At ten to ten I drove to the Safeway. I parked my car in the loading zone as close to the entrance as possible. I kept the motor running: there have been times when the car didn't re-start and Maura had to push. From my seat in the car I could see Maura strolling with Clare in the grocery cart. There were not many people shopping—it being early for Saturday. The conditions for the rescue were ideal.

Maura came to the section where the vegetables were kept. She picked up a huge squash and began examining it. "Buy it, you bitch, it's only thirty-nine cents a pound," I called out from the car. She did not hear me. She moved leisurely with the squash to a weighing scale suspended from the ceiling at the far end of the aisle.

This was the moment I had been waiting for. I dashed into the store, grabbed Clare from the grocery cart, kissed her, and ran back into the car. Maura screamed, as befitted her. What else happened I don't know. Within minutes I was in my apartment. My old car had behaved magnificently—it went faster than I had ever seen it go. God was on my side.

I put Clare on the floor and bolted the door securely. I moved the sofa against the door. I picked up the phone and, mustering as much courage as I could, dialed the police.

"Police Administration," answered a sweet voice.

"I want safe conduct for two to India," I said.

"Hold on," she said. The phone went dead for a minute. Then a male voice answered:

"Yes, sir."

"I want safe conduct for two to India," I repeated.

"Where are you speaking from, sir?"

"River Heights. Sixth Floor—suite 613. I want safe conduct for two to India."

"Your name, sir?"

"Tristan Elliott."

"Occupation?"

"Self-employed," I said to put him off the scent.

"Hum. Your phone number?"

"522—" I checked myself in time. It would be unwise to give away my phone number—the bastard was following up the trail. "Officer, just arrange safe conduct for two to India—quickly."

There was a brief silence, and then I heard what seemed like, "Looks like a kidnap—" It appeared the police officer was speaking to someone else. Then another man came on the phone, and every ten seconds I heard a beep on the line.

"Could we have the names of the persons for whom you are seeking safe conduct?"

"Clare and myself," I said. "And what's that bloody noise on the line?"

He did not answer. In an unruffled voice he asked her age.

"Sixteen months," I said.

There was a longish silence, punctuated by my "hello . . . hello." Then the voice came back.

"Clare's mother would like to speak to you. Would you . . . ?"

"Listen, mister, I have very little time and I don't want to spend it talking to her mother. I want safe conduct for two to India. Do you hear me?" I said with mounting temper.

"We'll be down in five minutes," he said.

"The door is bolted. Don't try any of your tricks. If you want to talk to me, come to the front of the apartment. Bring your megaphone—I have mine."

"Sir, where do you come from?"

"That's none of your business."

"Sir, please . . ."

"God damn you," I cursed and hung up.

My phone rang. It was the same chap. I hung up again. It rang again. I lifted it and put it off the hook. I then got into my subaltern uniform, donned the Castro cap and lit the cigar. I opened the window but kept the curtains half drawn.

I looked at Clare. She was squatting on the floor emptying my suitcase. "Darling," I cried taking her in my arms. She smiled and said, "Dada . . . Dada . . . Mama," and began to pull my nose.

I put her down near the Pooh bear and she began to stare at it as if it would bite her. Bright as she is, she first touched it gingerly on the back, and seeing that it did no harm she started playing with it. Meanwhile, I began putting my socks back into the suitcase. Suddenly it struck me that Clare's undoing my suitcase might be another omen from God—this time signifying that the rescue might fail. Already the police were responding in a fashion I had not expected. "Why doesn't God make up his mind?" I asked. Then I chided myself for trying to see God's meaning in every trifling incident. My nerves were taut—that's all.

"Mr Tristan Elliott." A voice came down from the street. So the police had arrived. I picked up the megaphone and going up to the window, said loudly, "Where are you?"

"Here," the voice answered.

I saw two men standing right below my window. One was much older than the other and they were both in civvies.

"Who are you?" I asked.

"We are police officers," said the older of the two. "I am Inspector Schudel and this is Inspector Nugent."

I looked at them hard. They were sloppy and wore their hair

rather long. Furthermore, there was no police car in sight. Whoever these two were, they were up to some mischief, I thought.

"You don't look like police officers! Where is your car? Where's your identification? Where's your megaphone?" I shot at them mercilessly.

They seemed floored. They looked sheepishly at each other with a smile on their faces connoting that they were exposed.

Just then two police cruisers arrived with their beacons flashing. Four officers got out and went up to the two men in civvies. They began to converse, and one of the uniformed officers said to me that the men in civvies would like to speak to me. I asked the officer who these people were and why they were not in their uniforms as befitted policemen on duty? He said they were hostage negotiators. Since I had taken no hostages I refused to talk to them. But I agreed to talk to the men in uniforms if they all moved further back and stood in the middle of the lawn and not under my window. I also insisted that they use the megaphone for all further discourse. They agreed without protest, and I could see that I had won the first round.

The uniformed officer, who had spoken to me earlier, addressed me on one of the two megaphones he fetched from his car:

"Do you have any weapon on you, sir?"

"What the hell do you think I am—a PLO?" I bawled, puffing at my cigar. "What do I need a weapon for? Though, by God, if I had one I wouldn't mind putting a bullet into one of you."

A couple of the policemen laughed, but the man who was addressing me remained serious.

"We would ask you to surrender the child. Kidnapping can be a very serious offence."

"I am not a kidnapper," I shouted at him. "A kidnapper flees from justice—he does not seek justice as I do. I contacted you to give me safe conduct for two to India. Say yes or no and don't waste my time."

"Sir, please keep your voice down. You'll soon get the whole district here."

"Nothing would please me better. Since when has rescue become a crime?"

"From what are you rescuing her?" asked the officer a little aggressively.

In top form as I was, the answer came to me spontaneously. I'm sure, though, it must have been in my mind for a long time.

"I'm rescuing her from duffers like you. I'm rescuing her from a society that is sick—a society that has deprived me of my wife, my son and my job and has put me on salary continuance insurance. I'm rescuing her from a society which has failed to exploit my potentials and refuses to recognize Clare's."

My stirring words sent the four policemen and the two men in civvies into conference again. On the fringes of the lawn people began assembling. A police van drove up with half a dozen policemen who set about cordoning off the area. It was I who spoke this time:

"I want safe conduct for two to India."

As the police officers did not respond, I continued, "I want two seats in the executive cabin of a British Airways 747. I want a window seat for Clare—I want to show her London from the air. I also have a few letters to write . . ."

As I was speaking, a car screeched to a halt. Maura jumped out and ran straight to the police officers in the middle of the lawn. She was followed by Dr Enright who, with his nose screwed up, looked disdainfully around him. Maura yelled at me.

"You bastard! You son of a pig! You give me back my daughter or I'll skin you. I'll kill you if you don't—you bastard!"

I heard every word she said, but it was my principle not to respond unless I was spoken to on a megaphone.

"Give her the megaphone," I said calmly.

On the megaphone she did not abuse me. She merely begged me to return Clare to her and said she'd do whatever I wanted.

I told her I could not possibly return Clare to her, at which she began to sob loudly.

The police officer interceded on her behalf. "Think of the mother. How can you think of depriving a mother of her only child?"

I thought for a while. The policeman was right. A mother is after all a mother, however bad she might be. And every child needs a mother. In Clare's case, however, I was as good as a mother. All the same I felt sorry for Maura. I said:

"Officer, arrange safe conduct for three! I'll take Maura with me. She can help me to build the hut and milk the goat. And in her spare time she can organize her Indian sisters to fight for their liberation."

I heard laughter from all sides. But Maura continued to sob hysterically.

"Don't, Maura," I said. "Your daughter is safe in my hands. Nobody dares disturb a hair of hers as long as I live. You'll be proud of her one day and you'll bless me for what I'm doing today. Your daughter is not your daughter, really."

"Give me back my child, give me back my child," she kept pleading between sobs.

"Ask for anything and I'll give it to you. Ask for a kingdom and I'll give it to you—but don't ask for Clare. Clare belongs to neither you nor me—she belongs to the universe. Come with me to India: we shall look after Clare together. Tell the policeman you are coming with me—ask for safe conduct. Tell them—"

I stopped in the middle of my sentence. I heard my name called several times. Martell in his dungarees was speeding on his bike in the direction where Maura, Enright, and the policemen stood. He held a paint brush in his hand, and a bucket of paint was suspended from the handle of his bicycle. The paint was splashing all over him as he rode roughshod over the pavement and onto the lawn. He got down, snatched a megaphone from a police officer and pushed the bike towards him to hold. Between gasps, he said:

"Tristan, stop it! Stop it! I say stop it! Don't ruin the good impression you have made in Kamsack. I tell you they'll never have you back again. Think of it. I know it! I know it! Stop it! I'll come up and get Clare. Hey, where are the stairs?"

I told him I wasn't permitting anybody to come up to my apartment and it would be better if he went about his own business. As for the good impression I left in Kamsack, I was prepared to sacrifice it for Clare.

"If you don't want me to come up, throw her down from the window and I'll catch her. I was once a baseball player, you know."

"Throw her from the window and you'll catch her! With your dirty hands! Haven't I told you not to go near Clare without washing the paint off." And I turned to the police officer and said, "Will you please send this nut away. I'm getting impatient, and at this rate we'll never board the plane."

I saw Enright talk to Martell and Maura. He must have persuaded them to leave, for I saw Martell place his hand on Maura's shoulder and lead her towards the police car. Behind the two a policeman walked with Martell's bike. Maura was still sobbing, but spasmodically. I was glad to see her go—I had come very near to giving up Clare when she cried, "Give me back my child."

The cordon seemed to have broken and people had made their way up to the lawn, though they still stood a little removed from the police. Among those I could recognize were Roxanne, shaking her fist at me; Sandy, Maura's baby-sitter, looking downcast; Edna, knitting a sock; Peabody, frowning and twisting his handlebar moustache, and the reporter from *The Hemisphere* with a camera round his neck. There was a TV crew as well, but neither the reporter nor the TV men were having much luck since the curtains were half drawn and most of the time I stood behind the curtains.

The person most conspicuous in the crowd was Ralph. He had on an old tweed jacket, khaki shorts and tennis shoes—but without socks. On his head was a shiny white cloth hat with the brim falling over his ears. He had a set grin on his face as he walked up and down, shaking hands with people and chatting with them. He seemed mightily pleased with himself and looked more like a candidate for mayor than a father about to lose his child. Perhaps he had faith in me—perhaps he was hoping I'd return from India with a wife for him. Occasionally he pointed in my direction while talking to his admirers.

"Ralph!" I called out over the megaphone. "How are you?"

He waved his hand affectionately and said, "Hi."

"Ralph, I'll send you—you know what?—from India. She'll be a real . . ."

"Shove it," he said quickly, the grin vanishing from his face. And he began walking away as if embarrassed.

"Do you want to see Clare, Ralph?" I asked to atone for my indescretion.

He did not reply, but the reporter from *The Hemisphere* jumped at the suggestion and asked me to pose for him at the window with Clare in my arms.

"To hell with you," I barked. "Your last photograph was, in the words of the Dean, 'a disgrace to the entire faculty.' You ought to be ashamed of yourself."

The reporter laughed and this threw me into a rage. "Get away from here," I shouted. "Officer, throw that rascal out immediately or I shall have no further dealings with any of you. It is your job to see that such undesirable characters stay out when important business in being conducted. I shall count thirty and if the man is still here I'll shut the window. One—two—three—"

By the time I had counted to twenty-two, the police had sent the reporter packing. A member of the TV crew then addressed me with marked civility:

"Sir, we hate to impose ourselves on you at such a time, but people across Canada are eager to know how the child is doing."

I turned around and saw Clare completely engrossed in her

play.

"She's playing with her Pooh bear," I said.

"She is not crying for her mother—is she?"

"Of course not."

"Sir, could we shoot a little scene with you and the child for our six o'clock news?"

"Yes, you may. I have nothing against the press as long as the press acts responsibly and does not disgrace the academic community. That reporter could have cost me my job—if I had one."

I parted the curtains fully and brought Clare to the window. Every eye was on us. Clare smiled and waved to the crowd and then began to pull my ears. People cheered and even the policemen seemed to relax. The only person who looked grim was Enright.

I put Clare back on the floor and returned to the window. The gentleman from the TV had one more question to ask. The police would not allow him, saying we must get on with the negotiations as it was already past twelve.

"Twelve!" I exclaimed. "It's Clare's feeding time! We must call off negotiations for fifteen minutes. Meanwhile you could arrange safe conduct for two."

"Sir, Dr Enright would like to speak to you. Could you wait a minute?" said the officer.

"Impossible! I'm sorry, but the baby must be served first. She should be fed at twelve—and now it is seven past twelve."

"Sir, sir . . . " pleaded the officer as I shut the window with a bang.

I opened a jar of fruit salad. After she had had salad, I heated some turkey with noodles for her. I then took off my shirt and vest and applied Marmite to my nipples. She sucked at my nipples for a full ten minutes and seemed to enjoy it more than the food. I wanted to reapply Marmite and prolong the suck, but the officer outside was begging me to talk to Enright. I also felt it necessary to complete the negotiations soon if I were to get on the evening plane. So I gave Clare her Pooh bear and opened the window.

Enright was standing, holding the megaphone to his mouth. I don't know how long he must have been standing in that position while I was feeding the baby.

"I'm ready, doctor," I said.

But he said nothing. He merely raised the megaphone a little higher—to position it in line with the window. Perhaps he was taking aim. I waited. So did everyone else.

I said at last. "I know, doctor, what you want to say. But let me assure you I've thought out the whole thing very carefully and there is nothing more to think."

"Think, Tristan, think. What you are doing will land you in prison."

"For what?"

"Kidnapping. You are kidnapping someone's child."

"On whose side are you?"

"On yours, Tristan. That is why I want you to give up Clare."

"Never, I shall never give up Clare."

"If you don't, I won't be able to help you, Tristan."

"I shall still remember you with gratitude. When Clare grows up, I shall tell her it was you who recommended the breast shield when she bit my nipples."

People tittered. Enright blushed and returned the megaphone to the officer and stood back, looking at the ground. It was Peabody's turn now. He walked up right under my window and standing with his hands on his hips and his legs wide apart, he began berating me. He called my conduct nauseating, disgusting, obscene. He asked the police where their sharp shooters were! I bared my chest and said that nothing would please me better than to die in the service of Clare.

"Shoot! Shoot!" I cried.

"Get me a gun," roared Peabody.

A policeman got Peabody to leave the premises. He swore he would have us all dismissed—the police first for their incompetence.

Peabody's outburst unsettled me, for I have respect for the

man's learning and know that he honestly cares for me. But what I found more disconcerting was the attitude of the police and the public. I had read that in situations like mine everybody gets more tense and agitated as time draws on. But here the opposite seemed true. Four hours had passed and the police seemed in no hurry to do anything. The police van drove away as if it were no longer needed. People were standing in small groups, talking and laughing and enjoying the sun. A few had spread newspapers and coats on the grass and made themselves comfortable. Someone had ordered Kentucky Fried Chicken, for a car (with Colonel Sanders painted on the doors) drove up to deliver the food.

The police came back on the megaphone again. They began taking turns now, but they all said the same thing: I must listen to Dr Enright; I must release Clare; there were no flights available to India for the next two weeks; they were prepared to discuss the matter with me if I would allow one of them to come up to my apartment. I was too clever to fall into their trap—and I told them so. I said I had enough provisions to last a month and I could wait a fortnight for the plane.

The negotiations had come to a standstill when Edna walked up to the police. After a brief exchange with them, she spoke to me:

"Tristan, I'm a mother of five kids."

"I know that, mother."

"I have another one here," she said patting her belly.

"God bless you, mother."

"As a mother, Tristan, I say you cannot take Clare away from her mother."

"But—"

Clare began to cry. I excused myself and turned to see what was the matter. The floor around her was wet.

"That's all right, my darling," I said. "I'll get you a fresh diaper."

I looked around. I had none! What sort of a mother was I? Of all things I had forgotten to buy diapers! I couldn't believe it! I felt lost. All my preparations seemed to have come to naught.

"Edna!" I gasped, rushing to the window.

"Tristan, what is it? Clare! Is she all right?"

"Edna, mother, I don't have diapers," I moaned.

"Is that all? I have a couple in my bag—you can have them."

"Thank God, Edna. You bring them up."

Before Edna could reply, the police officer took the megaphone from her. Dr Enright and the other policemen encircled her, and they all went into a huddle. I knew what they were up to and I smiled to myself.

The police officer spoke. "Edna is afraid to go up alone. She'll come with one of us."

"No, she won't," I retorted. And then I addressed myself to Edna: "Are you afraid to come up alone, Edna?"

Edna hung her head down and said nothing. So that was it. The police were up to their usual game.

"We'll send your doctor up with the diapers. He'll also examine Clare and see that she's all right."

"No, he won't. I won't allow any man up here. Only a woman can come up."

"Well, which woman?" asked the officer sarcastically. "How many women here do you know? And who's willing to go to your room alone?"

"He knows me. I'll go and diaper him," said big Roxanne with a swagger.

"You won't. You won't come anywhere near me. I know the sort you are," I said.

The people laughed, but not so the police. They certainly had hopes of tricking me—the fools!

"Well, sir, do you want the diapers or not?" asked the officer.

"Yes, but I am looking for someone to bring them up."

Just then Sandy, the baby-sitter, spoke to the officer, "I'll take the diapers up." And she asked me sweetly, "Tristan, will you let me come up?"

"Of course, Sandy. You more than anyone else." And I recalled how Sandy had driven me home after Roxanne had clobbered me. "You can also kiss Clare goodbye," I added, knowing how much she cared for Clare.

Sandy's offer had fouled up the police plan: I could see it from the frowns on their faces. They took her aside and began to talk to her in hushed voices. No doubt they were reprimanding her for coming up with an offer which deprived them of a chance to sneak into my apartment and subdue me physically—since intellectually I was so much their superior.

"Send her up, officer." I said triumphantly. "Today just isn't your day. And don't bully the poor girl! It was you who asked who'd come up to my apartment alone. You have the answer now."

The police made no reply but kept talking to Sandy. They were now joined by Dr Enright and Edna.

"Send the diapers up," I bellowed in the megaphone. "If I were a dictator, I'd let no man join the police force whose IQ was under fifty. You are all a drain on the public purse."

"Ya, ya," said someone from the crowd. But the police ignored him as well as my remark. They took the diapers from Edna and gave them to Sandy.

"Come up, Sandy. Take the elevator to the sixth floor and turn right. Mine is the last door—suite 613. Knock three and a half times and say 'Open sesame.' Make sure the police don't follow you because I'll check through the peep hole before I open the door."

Sandy left. I surveyed the entire scene like a monarch, and raising a clenched fist I shouted to the police, "To your tents, O Israel." Then I shut the window so they couldn't throw in a tear gas.

A minute later Sandy knocked. I looked through the peephole and saw her standing meekly. I pulled back the sofa and opened the door. I asked her in. She smiled and extended the hand holding the diapers. As I was about to take them, she let go the diapers, grabbed my wrist, punched me in the head, swept my feet from under me and kicked me in the groin. As I writhed on the floor, two men in plain clothes pounced on me.

I heard Clare howl.

"Kidnap! Kidnap!" I shouted as the men overpowered me. I called to the police for help, but they could not hear me. I had shut the window—a fatal mistake.

22

I have been admitted to a hospital for indeterminate injuries to my head. An armed police guard is posted day and night outside my door to protect me. Dr Enright comes to see me every morning. I ask him if there is any news of Clare. He shakes his head sadly, but tells me not to worry. The police know who the kidnappers are and will apprehend them one of these days.

Until they do—I cannot but worry.